Bloody Meadow

Bloody Meadow

Andy Johnson

Bloody Meadow

All Rights Reserved. Copyright © 2023 Andy Johnson

No part of this book may be reproduced or transmitted in any form or by any means, graphic, electronic, or mechanical, including photocopying, recording, taping or by any information storage or retrieval system, without the permission in writing from the copyright holder.

The right of Andy Johnson to be identified as the author of this work has been asserted in accordance with the Copyright, Designs and Patents Act 1988 sections 77 and 78.

This is a work of fiction; a dramatization of historical events.

The views expressed in this work are solely those of the author and do not necessarily reflect the views of the publisher, and the publisher hereby disclaims any responsibility for them.

Contents

Acknowledgements...........................xi
Foreword..xiv

Map 1: The Area of Operations......xvi
Map 2: The Battlefield xvii

The Arrival..1
The Arrow-storm 31
The Assault 63
The Rout..135
Epilogue 173
Historical Note 177

Acknowledgements

The excellent cover image is 'The Battle of Towton',
Copyright © Graham Turner, the artist, at www.studio88.co.uk

All maps are the author's own.

This book is for Harry Oldfield,
who first told me the story and walked the field with me;
and for Mrs Paver, who taught me history.

Foreword

Most people have heard of the Wars of the Roses, although very few know a great deal about them. They were, in effect, a series of interlinked civil wars and family feuds that dominated the political landscape of England for a period of around 30 years, from the mid-1450s to the mid-1480s. The original protagonists coalesced around two extended noble families, centred on the Dukedoms of York and Lancaster; although these names have no real implications in regard to geographical locations, ownership, or areas of support.

The Wars of the Roses were noteworthy for a number of reasons, not least of all the savagery of the fighting and the ruthlessness with which political rivals were dealt. A number of noble families would lose several generations of titled members killed within just a few years of each other, with fathers and sons often falling victim to the wars in rapid succession. The complex relationships between the noble houses and their extended family networks made for a dangerous mix, with betrayals and the changing of loyalties a relatively common occurrence.

The tone of the wars was set early-on during the initial, relatively small-scale battles and early manoeuvring where the practice of taking men of rank prisoner and then ransoming them was quickly abandoned in favour of summary execution. By 1461, the noble families on both sides of the argument already had numerous grudges laid against their rivals which acted as powerful drivers for revenge. Also, by this stage, the power struggle had reached the point where the heir to the House of York, Edward Plantagenet, was openly claiming the throne from the existing king, Henry VI.

The scene was thus set for a decisive clash of arms between the two sides. During a very active campaign, conducted in the depths of a bitter winter, both sides assembled what were probably the two largest armies ever put in the field in England up to that point in history, and most likely have not been surpassed since. Although medieval chroniclers were notoriously bad at counting and/or prone to exaggeration, it is clear that the scale of the campaign was something highly unusual for the time.

Following some preliminary actions, the two sides met on Palm Sunday, 29th March, 1461, perhaps rather unexpectedly, in the middle of a blizzard, on a desolate plateau that rises high above the North Yorkshire plain, just a few miles from the small town of Tadcaster. Several villages bordered the plateau, but the one which acted as the forming-up point for the Lancastrian forces was called Towton, and that small settlement gave its name to this most deadly of encounters. What followed that day would go down as the bloodiest battle ever fought on English soil. Tens of thousands of men fought a pitched battle for many hours, at close quarters, in the driving snow, and thousands of them were slaughtered both on the field, and during the rout that subsequently ended the battle.

If the date, the size of the armies, and the casualty figures weren't significant enough, the consequences of the battle were. The battle gave England a new king. Edward IV, who founded a new royal dynasty; the Plantagenets. Edward changed the history books that day upon the battlefield of Towton, and due to the vastness of the armies, and the fact that two thirds of England's nobility took part in the battle, it was a conflict which affected virtually every village, town, and city in England. This is the story of that fateful day; the story of Palm Sunday Field; the story of Bloody Meadow.

Andy Johnson
February 2023

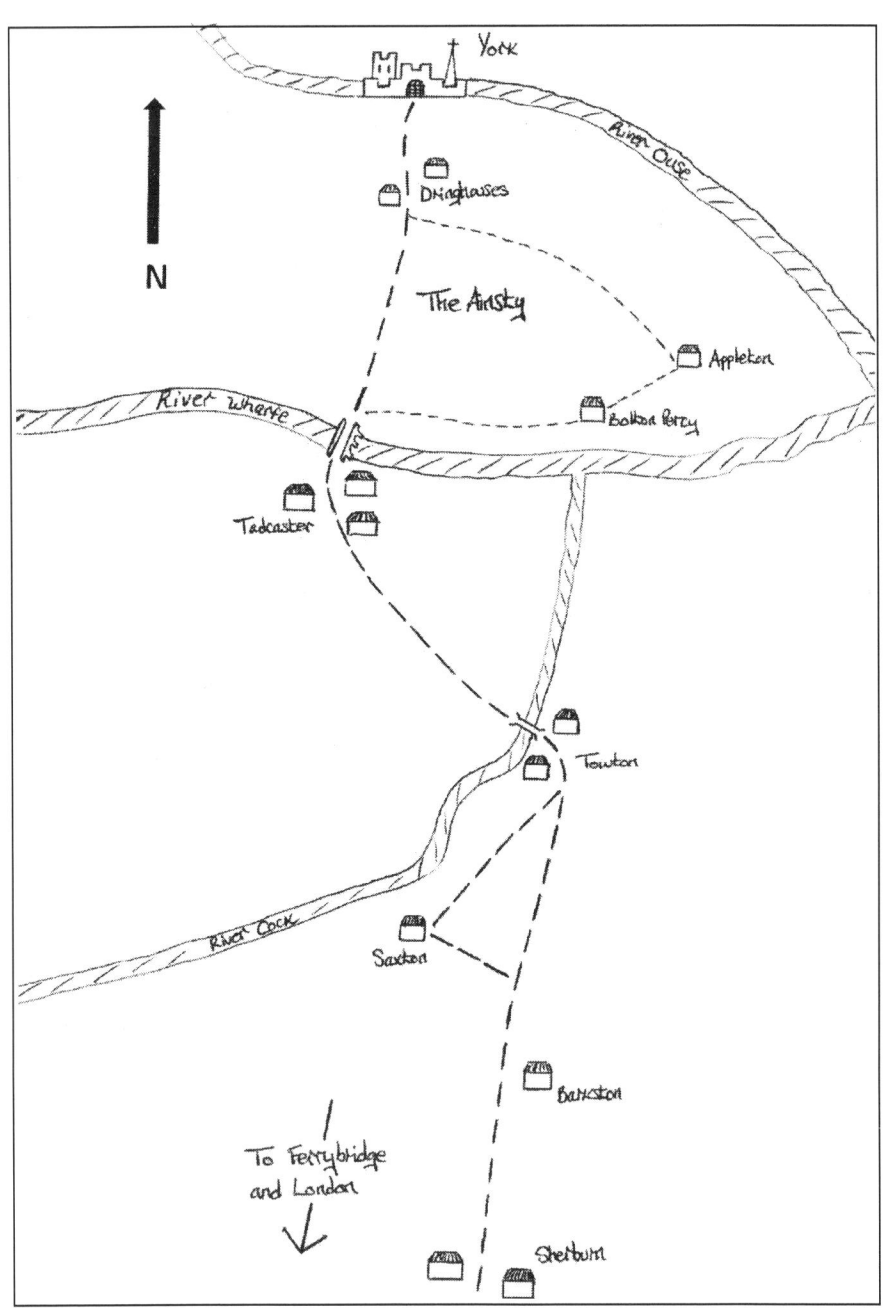

The Area of Operations

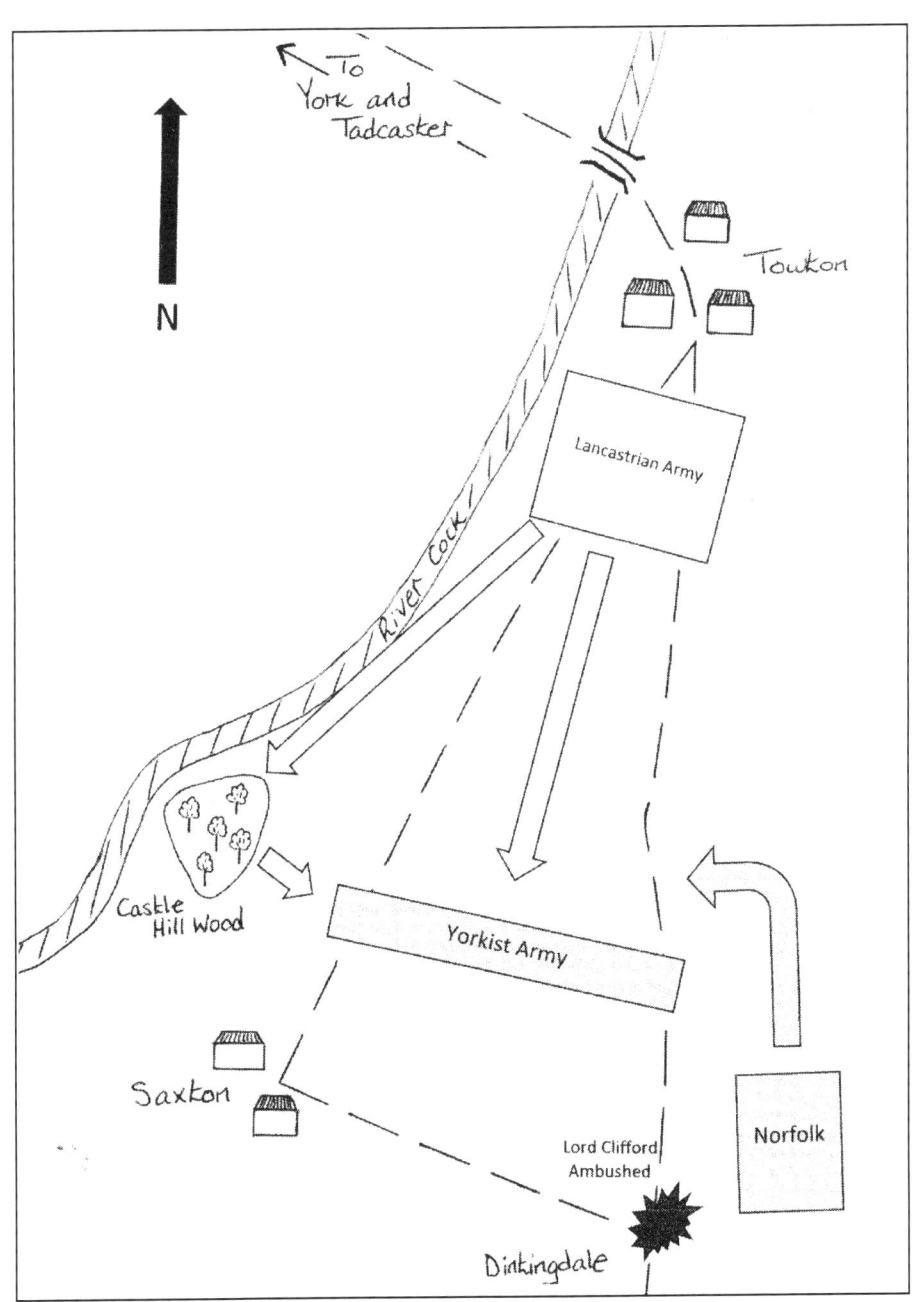

The Battlefield

The Arrival

It was a shitty day. The skies were leaden, and any person without good cause and with even a modicum of common-sense would be indoors, close by a warm hearth and swathed in thick wool. Unfortunately for John Clifford, the 9th Baron of Skipton and Lord of Craven, there was plenty of cause for him to be abroad.

A curtain of sleet descended, blown almost horizontally by the wind into the faces of the nobleman and his retinue. The Lancastrian warlord bent his head, dug his spurs into his horse's flanks and urged it onwards, though it stubbornly ignored him and continued on at a frustratingly slow trot. The beast wouldn't move any faster; not for a good while yet. It was completely blown from the mad gallop of the hasty withdrawal from Ferrybridge.

If it hadn't been for those Yorkist bastards of course, Lord Clifford, his followers, and indeed the entire Lancastrian army would have been safely tucked up behind solid castle walls; dry and warm before roaring fireplaces, surrounded by tapestries, and with the smell of freshly cooked food wafting through the passages and staircases.

But these were dangerous times; so dangerous that the King and Queen and their loyal followers from the House of Lancaster had been forced to take drastic action in the very depths of winter; a winter that was showing no sign of giving way to spring.

It had started so well. They had lured out that filthy traitor, Richard of York, from his castle at Sandal near Wakefield, and then fallen upon him in the open, boggy ground before the town. There they had trapped the rebellious duke and his followers and slain them in a short but vicious battle. York had been caught completely by surprise in the ambuscade and he had died like the treacherous dog he was, alongside his equally treacherous knights, captains, and followers. York's son, Edmund the Earl of Rutland, had died there too; killed by Clifford's own hand.

The seventeen year-old son of the great traitor had managed to break free of the slaughter, riding pell-mell for the bridge into Wakefield, seeking to make good his escape. However, a number of the lower class of Lancastrian footmen had blocked his way and caused his horse to rear-up. Thrown from his mount, Rutland had hit the ground, winded and disoriented; and there Clifford had caught up with him. In an act of pure revenge, prompted by his own father's death at the hands of the Yorkists five years earlier, and determined to extinguish the last sparks of Yorkist resistance, Clifford had killed the young earl in cold blood.

Despite the hard ride and the icy cold sleet, Clifford smiled maliciously as he remembered striking the death-blow and hearing Rutland's pathetic squeal as he died. His brief moment of satisfying reflection was short-lived however, and his smile faded.

The victory at Wakefield should have been decisive. It should have been complete. It should have been the end of the whole damned business. Indeed, it would have been were it not for Edward, Earl of March; eldest son of the now dead Duke of York. For Edward still lived.

He had been in the west, near Ludlow, at the time of the battle. Instead of fleeing abroad at the news of his father's death, the eighteen year-old, himself now inheriting the title of York from his slaughtered father, had reacted with fury. He had assembled an army, taking in reinforcements from other Yorkist lords who had marched to his assistance. Not long after, the fledgling Yorkist army had confronted a Lancastrian force marching from Wales, at Mortimer's Cross, and put them to rout with great execution.

And then Edward had turned south, first marching on London and drawing in followers from across the southern counties. From London, he had turned north, apparently intent on finding and confronting the royal army to seek vengeance for his slain kin. And that was why Clifford was riding, saddle-sore and bone-weary, through a blizzard of fucking sleet in a god-forsaken stretch of Yorkshire.

Hearing of Edward's approach, the Lancastrian council of war had dispatched Clifford and his men southwards as an advance-guard to seek out the advancing Yorkists and attempt to delay them. Meanwhile, the main Lancastrian force was re-assembling, drawing in as many extra men as possible from the surrounding countryside to fill out their ranks, before following on behind Clifford to find a suitable field of battle on which to confront the upstart Edward of York. There would be one more great battle, and this time the final treacherous adult dog of the Yorkist pack would be put down without mercy. Afterwards, Edward's head would join those of his father and brother on the spikes above Micklegate Bar, the main entrance into the city of York.

Again, Clifford smiled wickedly to himself as he pictured in his mind's eye, Richard of York's head wearing a paper crown, spiked there on Micklegate's tower, hung about with a sign that read "York looks upon York". That had been Clifford's idea too, which his fellow Lancastrian nobles had found highly amusing. The Queen had particularly enjoyed the pun, and he could still picture the smug expression she wore when she had first looked upon York's severed head.

The time was at hand. After years of struggle between the two great families in England, soon the kingdom would finally know peace, and the House of Lancaster would hold the reins of power completely and without challenge.

Thus far, the strategy had gone well. Clifford and his men had reached the River Aire at a small hamlet named Ferrybridge on the Great North Road, and there, much to everyone's surprise, they had encountered a Yorkist vanguard under Fitzwalter's banner, settling itself into quarters at the village and still in the process of setting out its sentinels.

Without pause, and with a wild fury, Clifford and his men had pounced on them. It had been like another, smaller version of Wakefield again. They had cut-down dozens of Yorkists, common men and titled men alike. Only when more Yorkist troops began to arrive in the village did Clifford and his men realise that the main Yorkist army was close behind their vaward and break off the action, doing their best to pull down the bridge across the river as they left.

Victorious and drunk on their small victory, Clifford and his men had thundered back northwards to find the royal army and let them know that the young pretender of York was on his way in full force. The rush of battle had now evaporated however, the Lancastrian horses were blown, and Clifford and his men were wet, cold, and shivering in the icy wind. It really was a shitty day.

As Clifford ruminated, the column of mounted men dropped off the slight ridge and into a shallow vale, and another hamlet came into sight. It was larger than most of those that were strung out along the main road between London and York, but no less mean. Most of the dwellings looked to be hovels, with just a handful of more respectable houses; though none of them matched the more robust and affluent town-houses to be found in the city of York, just twenty miles to the north.

The road here was a morass of mud and puddles, being as it was a crossroads of two major highways that clearly saw significant traffic. Clifford's horse kicked up huge blobs of filth as it stamped its way along the main street of the hamlet, and the three hundred horses that followed directly behind did likewise.

There were few people abroad; unsurprising given the weather. Peasants would take any opportunity not to go about their work, and a day like today was a perfect excuse for idleness. In the centre of the village however, one individual was crossing the main street as if heading towards one of the better houses. The elderly looking man immediately checked his pace as he heard the sound of the approaching column and looked up sharply.

For a moment, it seemed as if he might scuttle back the way he had come, but Clifford had already transfixed the man with his haughty gaze, and instead the villager simply stood there, rooted to the spot amongst the mud and filth of the road.

Clifford hauled on his horse's reins as he neared the man, and the feisty animal skittered impatiently to a halt. The Lancastrian lord stared down at the old villager who bowed his head obsequiously. From his appearance, the villager was one of the more senior freemen of the peasant class; probably descended from the ancient Saxon families who had once held sway in this land, and probably a bit of a somebody within this particular community. To the twenty-five-year-old Lord of Craven however, the man was a nobody.

"What is the name of this place?" Clifford demanded without preamble.

"Sherburn, My Lord." The villager gabbled quickly without meeting the younger man's gaze. "In the old country of Elmet, now part of the shire of York."

Elmet. An old name used for this part of the world since before the great conquest of 1066. Definitely of Saxon blood then.

"Have you any word of the King's army?"

"Aye, My Lord. The villager replied, his voice heavy with trepidation. It was difficult to know who fought for who in these dark days, and his uncertainty was evident.
"Riders from the King's army were here no less than two hours gone; prickers searching for victuals and news."
Clifford became alert.
"What did they say? Where is the army?"
"Not far yonder to the north, My Lord. They have encamped upon the high plateau by Towton village, and in the fields beyond, towards Tadcaster. 'Tis no more than two hours steady walk from here; straight along the York road."

Clifford felt a surge of relief. By horse, that would be thirty to forty minutes at the most. In his mind, he vaguely remembered the village near the high plateau from his original journey south. It made sense. The location would make a good site for a battle. Just as importantly, his own servants and baggage would be with the army. Within the hour he would be reporting his glorious deeds to his fellow Lancastrian nobles and warming himself by a fire in one of the hovels of Towton village.

"Stand-back." Clifford snapped at the man, putting his spurs to his horse again.
The beast snorted and lurched forward as the villager took several hurried steps rearwards. Clifford urged his mount onwards, through the village and up the other side of the vale towards thickening trees. Behind him, the dirty, exhausted men of his personal retinue followed on.

They trotted on, slowly gaining the high ground again and passing beyond the long, thin brown strips of the villagers' fields and into an area of scattered trees. After several more miles they passed through another tiny hamlet amongst a stand of ash trees that a local peasant claimed went by the name of Barkston. And then, just another mile or so further on, the trees began to thin again as the road dropped into another narrow, but deep vale.

At the edge of the trees, as the road reached the bottom of the valley, Clifford pulled his horse up sharply again. Before him the ground rose quite steeply and to a significant height. Just visible, in the very far distance, he could see buildings, and the late-afternoon sky was smeared with the black smoke from hundreds of camp-fires. Towton village, with its great plateau, stood before them, no more than two miles distant; and there, encamped in their thousands, were the remainder of the Lancastrian army.

Clifford raised both hands and levered off his helmet, exposing his face to fresh air for the first time in many long hours. Despite the damp and the cold, he took in a long breath, then glanced to his left. Beside him, William Venn, Knight of Craven, sat solidly astride his own warhorse, clutching Clifford's personal standard in one hand. Venn was one of Clifford's most trusted retainers, and thus had been given the honour of carrying his Lord's standard into battle. The red wyverns and gold rings upon a white field stood out brightly amongst the browns, greens, and metallic greys of the surrounding countryside and the mass of weary, mud-splattered warriors in their white surcoats that bore his wyvern livery badge.

"You see, Sir William." Clifford smiled. "The army is before us; encamped in a strong position, yonder. The Yorkists have been sorely wounded by our actions today. Let us now join our kin and prepare to meet the traitor Edward and his mainward; provided the dog hasn't skulked away back to London."

Venn laughed at his lord's grim jest.

"Ride ahead, Sir William. Let them see my banner and know that we are friends."

"At your command, My Lord." Venn responded, his voice sounding distant and hollow from within his helmet.

The knight urged his big horse forward, passing in front of Clifford and taking the lead of the column. Behind Clifford his tired men were slowly spilling off the muddy road and forming a large wedge in the bottom of the valley, directly behind their lord. They had spotted the distant smoke of the Lancastrian camp, and a grateful murmur of anticipation developed amongst the crowd of mounted men. They had been riding and fighting hard for twenty-four hours without break, but now they were just minutes away from some degree of comfort and security.

Clifford glanced over his shoulder, surveying his dirty, hard-faced men.

"The camp is before us. The King's army is at hand. Soon, my lads, you will have warm fires and food as reward for your fine actions this day…"

And it was just at that point that the first arrow flashed through the air, streaked past Clifford's eyes, and slammed into the rump of Venn's horse.

The standard bearer's charger reared up, whinnying in shock, and suddenly Venn was toppling backwards out of his saddle, his arms waving madly. Clifford stared in utter shock as Venn's armoured body landed heavily in the mud and shit of the road, followed a moment later by Clifford's standard. And then more arrows came slicing through the cold, damp air of the winter's afternoon, passing before Clifford's eyes with a menacing whisper.

Even as Clifford looked round in alarm, more arrows slammed into the packed press of horses and riders in the bottom of the small valley. Instantly, all was chaos. Horses reared and whinnied in terror. Riders fought desperately to keep control of their mounts, whilst others toppled from their saddles. Several horses were already down on their forelegs.

Something slammed into Clifford's own horse and it reared up. The Lancastrian noble let go of his helmet so that he could use both hands to steady his mount. The expensive helmet landed in the mud as Clifford fought to regain control of his horse which, after several heart-stopping moments, brought its forelegs down again and allowed itself to be steadied. As he brought the horse back under control, Clifford looked round again.

The air seemed to be alive with arrows, slicing without pause into the tightly packed column from all directions. He could see numerous men and horses on the floor, floundering in the mud. Men were drawing swords and turning their horses outwards in a defensive manner. And then he saw them.

Riders; dozens of them, bursting from the trees further down the valley and galloping across it in a wide arc. Instantly, he realized what they intended. They were trying to block the road and cut Clifford and his men off from the Lancastrian camp. Even as his mind made sense of the unfolding situation, Clifford's eyes spotted the banner. An enemy rider sat on the edge of the tree-line, perhaps one hundred yards away along the valley, clutching a brightly-coloured square banner emblazoned with a distinctive livery; white crosses upon a red field, with a blue star in the centre.

Even at this distance, Clifford recognized it. Fauconberg; the seasoned Yorkist commander. Twice Clifford's age, and with a lifetime of battle experience, the old captain was one of the most trusted Yorkist commanders; the kind of man who would be given command of the vaward. The banner denoted that these were indeed Fauconberg's men, but whether the old goat was with them was a different matter, and Clifford's eyes searched the treeline for any sign of the enemy Lord's personal standard.

Clifford cursed out loud. How had the old bastard managed to overhaul him in this weather? It made no sense. Had Fauconberg and his men grown wings and flown here from Ferrybridge? No matter. All that counted now was to get to safety. The King's army was just a short gallop away. Clifford looked back towards Towton, focused his eyes on the steep muddy track that ran up the other side of the valley and alongside the edge of the plateau. Gritting his teeth, the young Lancastrian lord pulled his heavy sword from its scabbard, then urged his horse forwards. It responded instantly, though skittishly, sensing the urgency and responding to the cacophony of nearby battle.

Clifford dug his spurs into the beast's flanks, and it broke into a lurching canter. He bent his head low, urging the horse up the track. Even as the tired beast struggled through the mud and attacked the slope, horses and riders appeared before them, emerging from both sides of Clifford's field of vision. He raised his sword and let out a defiant cry of rage. The riders were prickers; lightly armed spearmen and mounted archers; mainly used for scouting and pursuit. He was a trained knight, dressed in full armour. He would cut them down; assuming they didn't scatter in terror first of course. Besides, his comrades in the King's camp would surely hear and see the commotion of battle and come riding to his assistance with all speed.

As his horse fought its way up the slope, instead of scattering, the enemy riders pulled in close together, forming an impenetrable barrier of men and horses, ten wide. They levelled their spears, grim-faced, and Clifford felt his horse falter, shying away from charging home on the muddy slope. And then the arrows hit home again, three at least. Two hit the horse, sending it up on its hind legs again, whilst a third slammed into Clifford's exposed face, passing through his left cheek and embedding itself in the right.

Stunned by the impact, Clifford was unable to concentrate on bringing his terrified horse under control this time, and suddenly, with a horrifying sense of realization, Clifford felt himself falling backwards, completely unseated. It seemed to take forever to happen, but then he experienced the mind-numbing, body-crushing shock of hitting the floor on his back, dressed in full armour.

The pain was almost irrelevant compared to the way his body seemed to be emptied of all breath in an instant. He lay there, winded, shocked, barely able to comprehend what was happening. There was a loud rushing in his ears, as if he were stood beside a waterfall in full force. The noise was so intense that the other sounds of battle seemed to have disappeared completely. His stunned brain told him that he needed to get on his feet. He tried to move, but nothing happened. It was as if every ounce of strength he owned had instantly evaporated. He tried again but found he could barely lift one arm off the floor, never mind his entire upper body.

Then the faces appeared. He recognized them. The Yorkist prickers. Grim faces; ruthless faces; common faces; not a man of title amongst them. Three of them, dressed in dirty hauberks that carried the fish-hook livery badge of Fauconberg upon them. Clifford stared in horror as he saw all three of them raise their spears, with the long lethal heads pointing downwards. He tried to call out for mercy; to demand they ransom him.

"I am Clifford, Lord of Craven!" He wanted to scream, but his mouth was impaled by an arrow, and his mouth was filled with the metallic taste of blood, which even now was beginning to trickle into the back of his throat. No words came out; just a terrified gurgle. And it was at that point that Clifford knew he was going to die. For a brief moment he remembered the Earl of Rutland. Had this been how it had felt for him? The cold terror of knowing that the end was just moments away? Clifford could no longer breathe, for his entre throat was now filled with blood. He was drowning in it. The horror of it was beyond belief, and suddenly he was wishing that it would all be over.

A moment later, it was.

*

William Neville, the Lord Fauconberg, could smell the slaughter well before he could see it. The commander of the Yorkist vanguard was old in war, and the familiar, sharp, metallic tang of blood, mixed with the nauseating scent of punctured bowels, was familiar to him. It carried clear on the late afternoon breeze, overpowering even the stench of his sweat-lathered charger, and he knew that somewhere just up ahead was a scene of carnage.

He had been told already, by one of his excited retainers riding back from the confrontation, that his leading men had caught the Lancastrian contingent from Ferrybridge and cut them off from their main force, killing many. Now, as he urged his horse carefully down the churned-up slope of the shallow valley and clear of the trees, the sight before him met his expectations entirely.

It was a relatively narrow valley, just several hundred paces across. At the far side a steep slope led up to a large plateau, whilst far over to the east, that plateau fell away sharply, and the valley opened out onto a wide plain that was littered with trees and rough heathland. The valley bottom was a butcher's yard. Dozens of horses lay sprawled sideways across a wide area, and several hundred men lay among their carcasses; equally as dead.

The carpet of bodies was predominantly clad in white livery, though here and there one could also identify blue and white livery on some of the corpses. A low cloud of steam rose from the piles of dead humans and animals and, amongst the shambles, men wearing Fauconberg's blue and white livery scuttled. They shouted excitedly as they looted the dead; helping themselves to weapons, helmets, rings and coin.

As the Yorkist lord reined in and surveyed the grisly scene, a rider dressed in Fauconberg's livery approached him, urging his horse up the slight slope. Fauconberg recognised the man as John Slatte, a captain of his retained archers. Beneath the tight-fitting bascinet that framed his weather-beaten features, Slatte was grinning broadly, and in one hand he carried a lance adorned with an elaborate standard.

Slatte's horse was blowing hard as he urged it up-slope, but it responded to its rider's demands nevertheless. Moments later Slatte was sawing on the reins to bring his mount to a halt before his lord. Still grinning, Slatte tossed the standard and its lance onto the ground before Fauconberg. As it landed, the cloth, spattered by mud and filth, unfurled. Its heraldic devices were unmistakable; red wyverns on a white field. Clifford.

"We caught them, My Lord!" Slatte laughed wickedly. "The Butcher and his men! We caught them here before they could reach their camp. Almost all of them are dead. Just a few escaped our ambuscade."

Fauconberg looked down at the mud-spattered standard then glanced back into the valley towards the piles of dead.

"And Clifford? What of The Butcher?"

"Dead, My Lord." Slatte replied with glee. "Taken down by arrows and then finished off by our prickers."

Slatte turned and waved towards the brown smear of the London-York road where it curled around the contours of the valley slope.

"His body lies there, My Lord; over by the road. Dead in the mud."

Fauconberg grunted in grim acknowledgement.

"My nephew, Warwick, will be pleased for the vengeance we have wrought here. It will help the scars of his leg wound heal all the quicker. And My Lord, Edward the King, will be pleased that The Butcher that murdered his brother without mercy has paid the wages of his sin. This was a good day's work, Captain; our men did well."

Slatte beamed at his master.

Fauconberg turned his attention away from the valley bottom and looked towards the far slope of the valley. He saw how the York road climbed halfway up the plateau, then turned sharply to the right and followed its eastern contours. Somewhere in the distance, through the gloom of the darkening sky, he fancied he could see buildings and the odd twinkle of light. He sniffed the air, once again absorbing the foul stench of death and spilled guts. There was something else on the breeze however. Wood-smoke.

"Any sign of the main Lancastrian army yet?" He asked of Slatte, whilst continuing to strain his eyes into the distant gloom.

"Some of our men have seen fires in the distance, My Lord. I have sent prickers up onto the ridge to spy out the land beyond."

Fauconberg turned his head to the left and squinted up at the outline of the high ridge. There were perhaps a dozen men on horses already up there, and again he could make out the blue and white livery that marked them for his own men. They were riding along the crest of the ridge, backwards and forwards, gesticulating wildly.

"Let us go up and join them." Fauconberg directed. "I would see the lie of the land for myself."

The Yorkist peer urged his horse forwards, down amongst the slaughter in the valley bottom. The beast snorted and skittered with excitement as it drank in the scent of death. Slatte wheeled his own mount and followed on beside his lord, keeping half a horse-length back, as respectful custom dictated. Behind the two warriors, Fauconberg's personal standard-bearer followed on, with a hundred more mounted men-at-arms at his back.

All of the companies in Fauconberg's service carried his livery banner as a badge of their allegiance. They were simple flags of basic design. His personal standard however, was much more elaborate and distinctive, and followed him everywhere in the field; signalling his exact position to his men.

As they navigated their way through the carpet of dead, Fauconberg surveyed the scene with a measured, professional eye. He had seen many a battlefield in his time. This was a relatively small one, yet there were so many dead concentrated in such a confined space that the overall impact was unusually horrific. For the thousandth time in his life, he mused on how the notion of chivalry was an utter nonsense.

There was nothing glorious about death. Men and horses lay sprawled without dignity, limbs flung wide at impossible angles, their faces etched with the horror of death, frozen for eternity on their lifeless features. The ground, already churned up by the passing of hundreds of hooves, made muddy from the incessant sleet, was now lathered in blood. Arrows protruded from men, horses, and the ground; their pale-coloured goose feathers rippling in the breeze.

"You couldn't have caught them in a better place." Fauconberg observed with professional appreciation as he picked his way through the carnage. "You must have ridden hard to overhaul them."

"Anything to pay these bastards back, My Lord." Slatte commented humbly, grateful for the praise. "Though, in truth, I think Butcher Clifford got lazy. He clearly thought he had us beat back at the river. Over-confident I reckon. It was the end of him."
Fauconberg nodded agreement, then put his heels to his mount as they reached the steep slope of the valley's far side.

Up they climbed, in silence now, focused on guiding their horses up the difficult scarp. The horses snorted even louder as they put all their effort into the climb. It had been a long day for these highly trained beasts, and they were getting tired now. Fauconberg reached forward and patted his horse on its broad, muscular neck. "Almost there, boy; almost there. You've done well today. You can rest soon enough."

As they neared the crest, Fauconberg noted that it was punctuated by several ragged looking hawthorn trees. Beside one of them, a group of prickers sat astride their mounts, talking excitedly to each other and pointing northwards. They turned in their saddles as they saw Fauconberg's party approach. Recognising their lord, the three prickers dismounted rapidly and went down on their knees before him.

"What see you from this vantage point, goodmen?" Fauconberg asked as he walked his horse the last few yards onto the flat of the ridge.
"The enemy, My Lord!" Called out one of the prickers. "Over yonder, across the heath. A great mass of them."
Fauconberg reined in and gazed northwards. He was sitting his horse atop a wide ridge that ran a good mile or so to his left. Before him was a wide plateau, perhaps another mile in depth. In its centre, the ground dipped slightly before rising up a little again. And there, in the far distance, flickering brightly in the thickening gloom of this winter's afternoon, were the fires of the enemy. Dozens of fires. He could see a dark mass across the far ridge, and it seemed that the fires sprang from within that dark mass.

"That's a lot of Lancastrians." Slatte commented from nearby.
"It is indeed." Fauconberg agreed. "You can smell the bastards from here. There must be thousands of them. Clifford was so close."
"But not close enough, My Lord."

"No; indeed not." Fauconberg responded.
He was silent for a while, squinting into the wind, sweeping his gaze across the wide-open space before him.
"Never before have I seen a field more ready for battle."
"Plenty of room for archers." Slatte observed.
"Aye, plenty of room. I just hope we can fill it with the men we have. We need Norfolk and the rearward to join us as quickly as possible."

Fauconberg turned in his saddle.
"Take Clifford's standard back to the King. Send one of our best men; one who can speak clearly. Inform the King that his brother's murderer is dead. Tell him that we have killed many of Clifford's men. And tell him that we have found the main Lancastrian army. Also, tell him there are thousands of them. Beg him to march here with all his strength and at best speed. Let him know that we shall have the advantage of the ground if we move quickly. Tell him there will be a battle tomorrow if he wishes to fight."

Slatte bowed his head in acknowledgement.
"I shall see to it immediately, My Lord; with all expediency."
"And call your men off from their looting. There is no time for that now. We must claim this ridge and hold it. There will be a fight tomorrow, and we must fight it from here. Get all our men up on this ridge as quickly as possible; every company; every man. Plant our banners along the ridge and keep the enemy's prickers at bay should they ride forward."
"Aye, Lord. As you command." Slatte replied, then paused, casting his gaze across the plateau. "It's a rare place to fight, alright. And it looks like the Lancastrians have brought every man in England to the field. It will be some fight I think, My Lord."

Fauconberg nodded; his face dour.
"It will be a fight we will never forget, Captain. It will be a pure bloody murder of a fight. So… Go send to The King. Beg him come to the field… And quickly…"

*

There were two coaching inns in Tadcaster, the small town that sat alongside the River Wharfe. The river was the last natural obstacle between Towton and the City of York, and the London to York road bridged the narrow, but currently very swollen Wharfe, at the north end of the town. On this particular day, neither of those inns had any common travellers as guests. Instead, both establishments were crammed with the cream of Lancastrian nobility; the lords and knights of the realm who would lead Henry of Lancaster's army in the anticipated clash with the army of the young pretender, Edward of York, Earl of March.

In the larger of the two inns, which sat by the main road and not far from the ruins of the old castle, the most senior nobles from King Henry's army, including Lord Somerset, the titular field commander, had gathered around a large table before the hearth.

The mood was tense, not because of any particular disagreement, but simply because the Lancastrian nobility were becoming increasingly impatient for news of Edward of York's army. They had despatched Clifford and a large retinue of mounted men southwards, towards the River Aire, to scout for the approaching enemy, and to harass them as much as possible whilst also sending back warning of their approach.

Earlier reports had told the Lancastrian nobles that Edward was well past Nottingham and moving fast, and that he had gathered a significant force en route. Just as well then, that the pretender to the throne had chosen to march into the Lancastrian heartlands to seek battle.

It was one of those bizarre quirks of England's system of patronage that many of the lands situated in the county of Yorkshire belonged to nobles loyal to the Lancastrian cause. Having heard of the size of Edward of York's army, and hearing also of his desire to avenge his father and brother, the Lancastrian lords had stripped every last man they could find from their lands to supplement their existing retinues of retained men.

Their army was vast. None of the nobles in the room had ever seen so many men collected together under arms. They were on home ground, commanded the largest army that had ever been seen in England, and should have been confident. Regardless, the waiting was beginning to fray the nerves of even the most patient man in the room.

"I thought we'd have heard from Clifford by now." Somerset complained, pulling his fur-trimmed cloak tighter about his shoulders.

The hearth was lit, but on this especially cold evening the meagre heat it gave off did little to keep the chill at bay.

"The weather may well be delaying his messengers, My Lord." Soothed Sir Andrew Trollope, the experienced and highly competent soldier whose advice had given the Lancastrians their most recent advantage. "And that's assuming he's spotted York's army. The rain and sleet have been so bad these last days that York may not yet be as far beyond Nottingham as we think. I wouldn't be surprised if we had snow before long. It is a foul winter, to be sure. It is not easy to march an army in this weather."

Somerset looked across at Trollope who stood to one side of the hearth, a goblet of wine in his hand. The forty-year-old warrior looked as tough as his reputation spoke of him.

"Should, we move southwards to meet him?" Somerset asked. Trollope shook his head.

"I would not advise it, My Lord. Better to find exactly where he is before we blunder around the countryside with thirty thousand men in tow. At least here we are well victualled, and if we are to fight York, the plateau at Towton will be the best place to face him. Its southern ridge blocks the London to York road entirely. He will have to fight uphill if he wants to get through us."

Somerset pursed his lips and nodded his understanding.

"Yes; you are right, of course. Nevertheless, this endless waiting taxes me. The sooner we are to action the better. I would be rid of York once and for all. The rest of that bloodline is still in its infancy. Once Edward of York is dead, the remainder of that treacherous brood can be dealt with easily enough."

"Don't forget that bastard, Warwick, and his uncle too." Came a third opinion; this time from Lord Dacre of Gisland. "They will need to lose their heads also, to be sure there is no power-base left to which a new pretender can attach himself."

Around the table, there were murmurs of agreement.

"Our patience will be rewarded, My Lords." Trollope interjected. "We have a superior force, and the choice of ground. If York chooses to fight, it will be the end of him."

There were no murmurs this time. Just a series of nervous looks exchanged.
"They say York, or March, or whatever he's calling himself these days, is enraged over the death of his father and brother; like a man possessed." The Earl of Northumberland intoned darkly.
"Possessed by the devil, perhaps; with whom he will shortly share residence…" Trollope responded confidently.
There was no chance for any other reply, for at that moment the door to the inn burst open, startling the group slightly. A sentry stepped into the room and held it wide for another newcomer who followed behind him. A moment later, a big, heavily cloaked nobleman stepped across the threshold. As he did so, the newcomer threw his cloak open flamboyantly, revealing a crimson livery on which were emblazoned three golden lions; the tunic edged in blue with gold fleur-de-lis. Henry Holland, the third Duke of Exeter, surveyed the open room and its occupants with a serious expression.
"York is here." He announced.
As one, every Lancastrian lord around the table shot to his feet in alarm. Even the phlegmatic Trollope set down his goblet on the table and turned to face Exeter with a face that had gone ashen.
"Here?" Somerset asked, his voice full of dread.
"At Towton. His vanguard is on the southern ridge of the plateau. We have seen the banners and personal standard of Fauconberg; and wherever Fauconberg is found, York will not be far away."
This latest information resulted in a flurry of urgent questioning.
"How is Fauconberg on the plateau? Where is Clifford?"
"Dead." Exeter said bluntly, stopping the racket in an instant. "Or at least that's what the survivors of his retinue told me. Clifford and his men had come across the Yorkist army crossing the River Aire at Ferrybridge. Clifford attacked them with some success and killed Lord Fitzwalter in the process. But the remainder of the Yorkist army then crossed the Aire upstream and threatened to cut Clifford off, so he withdrew at speed. Alas, the Yorkist vanguard caught him just a mile or so before Towton and attacked him in a place called Dintingdale. Most of his men are dead with him. Just a few survivors fought free of the ambuscade and reached our picquets by Towton village. And now

there are Yorkist banners and mounted men on the far ridge, just above the village of Saxton. There will be a battle tomorrow, My Lords; I am sure of it."

"Damn Fauconberg!" Swore Northumberland. "Why did we not occupy the ridge sooner? And how did he get here so fast? Can the man fly?"

For long moments, there was absolute silence in the room. Eventually, Somerset spoke; his voice low and filled with gravity.

"No matter. To arms, My Lords. We will move the middle and rearward up towards Towton tonight. York is come to the field. In the morning, we shall end this business… once and for all."

*

Edward, Earl of March, de facto Duke of York, and newly proclaimed King Edward IV, was a striking figure. Tall, handsome, and well-made, at eighteen years of age and just shy of his nineteenth birthday, he was in the full flower of youth. Despite a day spent in the wind, rain, and mud, his face was flush with good health and he exuded powerful, decisive energy.

The fire that had been brought to life in the hearth of the miserable little house in Sherburn gave his cheeks an even rosier appearance, and the light reflected in his large, lively eyes. Still dressed in his mail and upper plate armour, all beneath his distinctive blue and red livery, he stood now in the centre of the room, staring fixedly at Fauconberg's messenger.

Kneeling beside him, his nervous page was busy removing his master's leg armour, conscious that he was suddenly privy to a conversation of great magnitude.

"We have caught them, you say?"

The newly-proclaimed king, having asked for clarification, stared expectantly at the old knight in Fauconberg's service who had arrived just moments before.

"Yes, My Liege. Clifford and his men, who fought us at the bridge. We caught them not four miles north of here. To a man they are all dead, including The Butcher himself. My Lord Fauconberg sends you this token and says that your brother is avenged."

With that, the old warrior threw the long staff with its now muddied standard down on the rush-covered earthen floor.

Edward stared down at the heraldic standard of Clifford, Lord of Craven, with his bright, intelligent eyes.

"Partly avenged…" He murmured, almost to himself. "There are others yet to be punished for their murderous crimes…"

"My Lord Fauconberg says that you will have those others too, My Liege…" The knight continued, "…if you march to him by morning. The entire enemy host is before us, not more than a mile beyond where The Butcher was killed. There are thousands of them, My Leige. The northern horizon was black with the smoke from their fires."

The young king, forgetting the ministrations of his page, took several steps closer to the knight, who dropped his gaze instinctively. "Four miles, you say?"

Not more than that, My Liege. You follow the road north, through a tiny peasant hamlet called Barkston, and as you come out of the trees a mile beyond it, the field is before you."

"Is it a good place to fight."

"Lord Fauconberg says it is the *perfect* place to fight, My Liege; a vast plateau with room to array the entire army. Good ground for archers, with the flanks protected by steep slopes and softer ground. He begs that you come to the field with all your strength by daybreak, My Liege, for he is sure there will be a battle come the morning, and for now we have the advantage of the ground."

Edward listened carefully to every word. Then, when Fauconberg's man had finished, he looked across at the other two men of rank in the room. Richard Neville, Earl of Warwick, had just arrived only minutes before, in great pain and with his leg heavily bandaged from the arrow wound he had suffered at Ferrybridge earlier that day. He sat on an old chest, wrapped in a heavy fur cloak, his injured leg stretched out before him; a pained expression on his face. Beside him stood Sir John Conyers, one of Warwick's most trusted captains.

Without being invited to do so, Warwick spoke.

"The army is tired after this morning's fight and the march here. It will be nearly midnight by the time the last men arrive. The guns and baggage are unlikely to arrive before dawn. The mud slows them so."

Edward accepted the statement without emotion. After a moment, he spoke again.

"Norfolk?"

It was Conyers who spoke this time.

"Still half a day behind, My Liege; maybe a full day. I dare say he reached Pontefract this day. Perhaps we should wait for him…"

The Yorkist king was silent for a moment, pondering. He looked back to Warwick.

"You are in no fit state to stand in a battle-line, My Lord of Warwick."

A look of mild indignation crossed Warwick's face.

"I have marched the length of the country to fight beside you, My Liege. Let no man say that I deserted my liege-lord on the day of battle. I will tarry with him that will tarry with me."

A grateful smile spread across Edward's face.

"I know your loyalty and your bravery, Lord Warwick, and it is appreciated. But you would last only a heartbeat in the line with that limp, and I cannot afford to lose any more of my peers as I did Lord Fitzwalter. You must stay here, Warwick. Stay here and organise the march to the field. Send everyone forward, and then send on the guns and baggage when it arrives. Allow no man to be idle whilst Fauconberg faces the enemy alone. Drive the army on for me."

Edward turned back to the messenger.

"Good knight… The place where Lord Fauconberg faces the men of Lancaster; does it have a name?"

The knight glanced up.

"It lies between two mean places, Sire. Lord Fauconberg is positioned in the fields of a small hamlet that the peasants call Saxton. The enemy are encamped a mile further north, in the fields around a village called Towton.

Edward acknowledged the information with the slightest of nods, then turned back to Warwick and Conyers.

"My Lord Warwick… Oversee the assembly of our troops here as they arrive. They may stop to rest by the roadside but there is to be no encampment. The entire army must march to join Fauconberg by dawn. I will ride ahead well before that. The army must be marching from here by the second hour of the day. Sir John, you will bring up the mainward whilst My Lord of Warwick pushes the rearward up behind you. I will meet you at the field with Fauconberg and show you to your position."

The King fixed Warwick with a serious look.
"And one other task, Warwick… Send to Norfolk. Send riders along every road to the south. Find Norfolk, and tell him that he is to march his men northwards through Sherburn and onwards without pause. No stopping. Tell him to keep marching until he finds us facing the enemy… Tell him to find us upon Towton Field."

*

Mundric of Appleton was cold, miserable, tired, and very, very frightened. And with every step further away from his home village, his fear and anxiety grew. Pressed in on either side by other men from his home village of Appleton and other nearby settlements, he shuffled onwards through the darkness, his feet squelching in the freezing cold mud of the London road, which was, in effect, nothing more than a ribbon of quagmire; one that had already been churned up by hundreds, if not thousands of feet and horse's hooves.

Crammed into the centre of the mass of men, he was at least somewhat sheltered from the icy wind that was blowing from the north. Nevertheless, it was a foul night, and his misery was made all the worse for knowing that his own home, small hovel that it was, lay just four or five miles away behind him, across the River Wharfe and eastwards from the town of Tadcaster.

He glanced to his right and, in the gloom, made out the large, ugly features of Grimwald, another man from his village, but unlike Mundric, one who had served in their lord's retinue before. To his front, several other men from nearby villages such as Bolton and Colton trudged dutifully before him. Beyond them he could vaguely make out the bulkier forms of men at arms; common men like him, but part of the more heavily armed City of York militia.

Even in the dark, they were easily marked out by their padded jacks, smart surcoats of blue and white adorned with a white rose, and modern helmets. With the King in residence in York, the city corporation could do nothing else but respond to the commission of array they had been served, and they had duly provided almost a thousand men, all kitted out in a uniform manner; half of them armed with longbows, and the remainder with bills.

To Mundric's left was another man who, though from the Vale of York, was not from one of the villages that sat in the tight little corner of land between the Wharfe and the Ouse. John Fletcher of Bishopthorpe was a junior captain in the pay of the Percy family, to which all of the men around him owed feudal service, being as they were, tenants on Percy land. As Fletcher's name suggested, he was a man of the bow; not an occasional levy like Mundric who, like all his company, was an ordinary man of the land, pressed into service on the promise of pay and reduced rents, and on the presumption that he had complied with the law and spent his days of youth practising with the long war bow. Fletcher was a professional soldier, permanently in the pay of the Percy's. It was he who had trawled the local villages of The Ainsty, raising troops for the Lancastrian lord; he who had ordered Mundric to find his bow stave and assemble at the village cross.

Ordinarily, a feudal levy would have required no more than one or two men per village, normally taken in strict turn as dictated by the village squire, or through volunteering. Not this time however. There was much division across the country, and all the great lords of the kingdom were assembling to settle their differences. Travellers had already spread word of the death of Richard of York, and of battles fought in places far away that Mundric could only dream of. But three days ago, the entire countryside had been scoured by the men of the great Lancastrian lords in the name of King Henry himself; a commission of array being read aloud in every village.

A large number of able-bodied men had been called to arms; three times the usually levy. It was said that a great battle was in the offing. Thus it was that Mundric and his fellows had found themselves camping out in the freezing mud around Tadcaster these last two nights; the mantel of soldier thrown upon them. Mundric could use his bow of course, but not with the same skill that professional men of war such as Fletcher could use their weapons.

The captain looked the part. He wore a heavily padded jack, reinforced with metal plates stitched down the arms, and with large metal studs embedded at key points across the garment. He wore a steel bascinet and a spread of mail about his throat, and besides his bow and bag full of arrows, a short sword and knife hung from his belt.

Mundric and his fellows were, by comparison, barely dressed. They stood in their ragged labourer's clothes, with a thin smock draped over them, which bore a small heraldic badge on the left breast, marking them out as Percy's men. His only headdress was his leather cap, and besides his own bow and arrow supply, the only other equipment Mundric carried was a small hunting knife.

Now, Mundric and his fellow levies were part of a vast army of men, trudging clumsily through the dark, along the old London road, towards a nearby village where, it was said, the battle would be fought. Why they were marching in the middle of the night, he had no idea exactly, but nevertheless, the whole army was on the move. The night was filled with the stamping of feet in puddles, the squelch of mud, the sound of metal clanking metal, heavy breathing, and much cursing.

"What's going on?" Mundric wondered aloud. "Where are we going in the middle of the night?"
Beside him, Grimwald muttered a reply.
"They say there's going to be a battle."
"In the dark?"
"In the morning." The older man replied. "Not far away; next village up... So they say."

Mundric dwelt on that for a moment.
"I wonder who we'll be fighting?"
"Men of York, of course." Grimwald grunted.
Mundric pulled a face in the darkness. The City of York was behind them, ten miles away. It didn't make sense to him. As if reading his mind, Grimwald elaborated.
"The lords of York have come north to capture the city that carries their name."

Mundric marched a few more slippery paces.
"Do you think they'll really want to fight?" He asked, hoping that his companion would allay his fears and suggest that this was all just an exercise in bluff and double bluff.
"Oh, aye; certainly they'll fight. There's bad blood between all the lords. After what happened to the older York at Wakefield, there's sure to be a fight. Grudges to settle, you see..."

Again, Mundric ruminated. He didn't want to get involved in anybody else's arguments. He just wanted to be home, in his humble little hovel, with a chance of seeing Agnes, a girl from Bolton village he was especially sweet on. He had planned to walk to Bolton to attend the Palm Sunday service there, where he knew he would see her with her family. Instead, he was here, amongst an army of pressed men and grizzled professional warriors, all trudging through the mud in the darkness of a bleak winter evening, with nothing but death on their minds.

*

Jack of Hornby, his body trembling with cold, stamped his foot down on the thin branch and was rewarded with a satisfying 'crack' as the long finger of hawthorn snapped clean in two. Working quickly, he repeated the action, breaking the various sections of branch down into useful sized pieces of firewood. It was greenwood of course, so would smoke badly, but it would burn, and on this freezing cold, wind-swept hillside, any warmth at all would be welcome.

"That's it, Jack; get in on the fire. Let's get it going good and proper."

Kneeling on the frozen ground a couple of paces away, Jack's father, Will, was busy trying to coax the meagre flames to spread from the kindling to the larger pieces of fuel that had already been built around a central vertical prop. There were at least two other groups of men from their own company of archers making similar attempts at producing fire to stave off the bone-aching cold.

As far as the eye could see to the left, amongst the gloom of early evening, the mounted archers from a dozen or more different lords and knights had each taken post on a section of the high ridge, from where they could view the Lancastrian camp across the wide plateau; each and every group desperately trying to kindle flame for some semblance of warmth on this bitterly cold night.

Jack and his father, along with their landlord, Sir John Conyers, a knight in the service of the Earl of Warwick, had arrived on the field less than an hour since. The personal retinue of Lord Fauconberg and those of several of his knights had arrived well before them, and the evidence of the battle they had fought was horrifyingly fresh in the valley bottom. Sir John had conferred briefly with Fauconberg on his arrival at the field, and then sent the word to his captain of archers to deploy up onto the high ridge to support Fauconberg's own men. The main Lancastrian army was within sight, they were told, and the high ground must be secured and protected.

So now, Jack and his father, along with their fellow longbowmen, worked like demons to build a fire large enough to offer some comfort on this exposed ridge, where they knew they would have to spend the night without any additional shelter. And all the time while Jack snapped the branches and added them to the growing blaze, he kept one eye on the numerous fires that glowed bright in the gloom, less than a mile away across the plateau.

"How many do you think they have over there?" Jack asked of nobody in particular.

His father, blowing into the pyramid of kindling in an attempt to grow the flames, paused briefly and looked up at his son with a shrug. "Who knows? Not that it matters. The new king is keen to fight, so they say. There'll be a battle tomorrow regardless, I reckon. I just hope the rest of our army can catch up before the fighting begins."

His father's words were of no comfort, and Jack eyed the distant Lancastrian fires with increased worry. What if they came tonight, in the dark?

This wasn't his father's first campaign of course. Old man Will had marched with Sir John on two occasions before, but this time the knight on whose land they were tenants had stripped every village bare of fighting age men, including Jack. The talk amongst the company was of a huge battle in the offing and every lord and knight across the kingdom was contributing every man they had, to one side or the other. Exactly who one ended up fighting for very much depended on the loyalty that one's own master held for either the House of York or Lancaster.

The system of feudal patronage meant that most common men had no choice whatsoever. Squires and professional captains owed their allegiance to knights, who in turn owed allegiance to a particular noble, who in turn chose to fight for one of the two kings currently claiming the English throne. All a common man could do was stick

close to his fellows from his company and fight as hard as possible in the hope of victory and survival. Avoiding defeat was all that mattered. In these wars, there was little in the way of honour or mercy, and common men counted for nothing. They were dispensable at whim.
"Cheer up, Jack."

His father's words snapped the younger man's attention back to the fire.
"We'll do all our fighting from a distance with the bow. Sir John's men-at-arms will do the heavy work with their bills. And besides, you see that old boy that Sir John was talking to earlier? That was the Lord Fauconberg. He's an old warhorse. Been fighting since he was a bairn. They say there is no finer commander in England with an eye for the battlefield. If he's on our side, we'll be alright."
"I heard Warwick was wounded this morning." Jack replied, only marginally reassured.
"I heard that too." Interjected Edgar of Fernbrough, another archer in their company. "Though they say it is merely a slight wound from an arrow."
"Aye..." Will agreed. "I'd heard that too. He'll still be able to command from a horse, and he has knights a-plenty in his service who can act for him. All we need to remember tomorrow is, follow the Captain's orders, and stay close to Sir John's banner."

Jack glanced round the group of half a dozen men gathered about their small fire, shivering in the icy wind. Like him, they all wore their own clothing; although a couple of the older men like his father wore padded jacks made from dirty white cloth. All of them had small livery badges sewn onto their left breast. The livery badges had been given out on behalf of Sir John; small squares of white hessian on which were painted a series of red crosses, with each arm crossed again by a smaller bar.

Almost every man in the army wore such a badge, of various designs, to identify the knight or lord under whose banner they fought. The ranks had been so swollen by the extraordinary recruiting effort, that only a handful of men wore full livery surcoats. For the remainder, the small cloth badges sewn onto personal clothing would have to suffice.

A particularly strong gust of wind blew across the ridge, threatening to extinguish the embryo blaze, and sending a shiver down Jack's spine.
"It's going to be a cold night." He grumbled.
"It is, lad." His father agreed. "And I reckon there could be rain or even snow before dawn. So, for now, forget Harry of Lancaster and his men over yonder, and get some more wood on this fire. Or we'll all freeze to death before we get a chance to fight anyone."

The Arrow-Storm

William Neville, the Baron Fauconberg, stood patiently by his horse. Around him were more than thirty other men, all dismounted and holding their horses by their bridles. About half of them wore Fauconberg's own livery; the remainder were in the blue and red livery of Edward, Earl of March, and now nominally King Edward IV and head of the House of York. The King was at prayer with his private chaplain inside the small church in the village of Saxton, which sat nestled in the small valley behind the ridge on which the Yorkist army was forming up.

The army had begun arriving late the previous evening; in dribs and drabs at first, but then with an ever-increasing regularity. The light horsemen, mounted archers and prickers, had been the first groups to arrive; every company from every knight and lord in the army, sent on ahead by Fauconberg's nephew, Warwick, in order to get as many troops onto the ridge above Saxton as possible lest the enemy sally out from the opposite, narrower ridge, on the edge of Towton village.

Then, in the early hours of the morning, Edward had arrived with his personal retinue to consult with Fauconberg and discuss the coming battle. Hard on his heels had come the bulk of the army. Division by division, retinue by retinue, they had come trudging through the deep mud of the London-York road in the first growing light of dawn. Mounted knights in full armour, with their colourful coats-of-arms emblazoned on surcoats, each leading yet more archers on foot, along with the solid blocks of billmen and pikemen who would form the main battleline. Above all these retinues flew the livery banners of the noblemen to whom they were indentured.

It had been a strange sight. The army was soaking wet, caked with the filth of the muddy roads along which they had marched at speed; the faces of the men white and sickly with exhaustion and exposure to the harsh weather. Yet, despite this, they were emblazoned with every colour and heraldic device one could imagine. Reds, blues, greens, and yellows; bears, lions, griffons, ragged staffs, and in the case of Fauconberg's own retainers, fish-hooks. The colours and emblems told the story of this battle more than anything else.

The whole of England had come to this windswept plateau in the county of Yorkshire to do battle. It was going to be an epic struggle, from which only one army would emerge in any semblance of order. Fauconberg was old enough to realise the truth of what was about to happen. This would be no skirmish. This would be a climactic end-game. There would be one winner, and one loser... and woe betide the loser.

The doors of the small church creaked, and a moment later swung open. Two of Edward's bodyguards stepped into the half-light of dawn, and a moment later the boy-king himself emerged. Tall and sturdy already at the tender age of eighteen, Edward's face was a mask of resolve. Behind him, his personal chaplain followed quietly in his wake. The King was in full armour. The metal scraped free of rust by his page in the night had already begun to show signs of spotting again around the rivets, such was the foulness of the weather. His surcoat bore his personal coat-of-arms upon a blue and red field. He looked like a king. Let's just hope, thought Fauconberg, that he can fight like a king too.

The assembly bowed low as Edward emerged into the street of the shabby little village, and his charger, recognising it's master, snorted impatiently and stamped as a groom tried to hold it steady.
"My duty to God is done." Edward announced, looking straight at Fauconberg. "Now my duty to my family and to England must be done. We shall inspect the lines, my Lord Fauconberg."
"At your command, My Liege." The old warrior bowed again in acquiescence.
He waited for the King to mount his charger, then, along with the remainder of the party, Fauconberg mounted his own horse.

They rode together, side-by-side, their retainers trailing behind them, up the narrow track which led to the plateau and on towards Towton. As soon as they left the relative shelter of the hovels in Saxton village, the wind cut through them like an icy knife.
"A hard day for a fight, Fauconberg." Edward observed.
"A hard day for anything, My Liege." Fauconberg agreed. "But it's no bad thing. Fighting keeps you warm. The men will be eager."

Edward glanced at the old soldier to gauge whether he was jesting or not, but Fauconberg's face was expressionless. Around them were thousands of men. Most of them were already up on the ridge itself, but there were many others still being formed into companies and chivvied by their captains; being forced away from the relative comfort of their small fires. Wood smoke lingered on the cold, damp air, creating an artificial mist.

"Yes..." Edward acknowledged. "The men will be glad for the business of the day. Anything rather than sitting out in this weather." Fauconberg glanced toward the young king, finally allowing a faint smile to cross his weather-beaten features.

"The weather may yet do as a good turn, My Liege." He suggested cryptically.

They were nearing the crest of the ridge now, and Edward looked away to raise his hand and acknowledge a ragged cheer that had begun to ripple along the rear ranks of the forming Yorkist troops. Men turned and spotted the royal party and began dropping to their knees, crossing themselves and shouting blessings, and all the other little rituals of submission that were as natural as breathing to the common man.

The party reined in at the top of the ridge, directly in the gap between two companies of archers. Edward scanned the wide plateau before him, trying to make sense of what he could see in the first light of dawn.

"Tis a big field." He remarked.

"Very big, Sire." Fauconberg agreed. "I fear we may be stretched quite thinly until Norfolk arrives."

Edward looked at him sideways.

"You think we should wait for Norfolk?"

"No, Sire." Fauconberg shook his head quickly. "Please do not mistake me. We cannot expect the men to stand around in this weather. They are cold, and wet, and tired, and hungry. Leaving them to wait would take the spirit out of them. We must fight, and trust in Norfolk joining us at best speed."

The old warrior pointed off to the left.

"You'll see a wood over yonder, My Liege. That marks the edge of the plateau. Beyond it the ground falls sharply away to a river known locally as The Cock Beck..."

Fauconberg twisted in his saddle and pointed in the opposite direction.

"And over there you will see several hawthorn trees. The furthest one marks the edge of the plateau again. From there, the ground drops steeply over the London road and away into fenland and woods. By these two features, we can anchor our line."

Edward nodded his understanding.

"But we must attack the enemy, My Lord Fauconberg, surely?" Edward gestured across the plateau where a dark shadowy mass was slowly revealing itself to be the entire Lancastrian army.

"Look how many men they have across there. I fear they outnumber us, and their ridge seems to be narrower than our position here. Their army is packed in a tight block on commanding ground. Surely they will stand there and await our attack, and benefit from the advantage?"

"Indeed, My Liege." Fauconberg allowed. "Unless of course, we can persuade them to come to us."

Edward frowned, just as a chill blast from the south swept a wave of freezing cold air and snow-flakes across the ridge.

"Why would they leave such a strong position when it is us that must seek the advantage? Why would they come to us?"

Fauconberg turned to squint into the wintry squall and allowed a smile to cross his wily features.

"Because, Lord King, the wind has changed direction, and I have a plan..."

*

Henry Beaufort, Third Duke of Somerset, glared out across the wide plateau towards the long dark smear on the far ridge which indicated the position of the Yorkist host. He was tired, irritable, and cold. The freezing wind had picked up speed and was blowing from the south-east, right into his face, and with it came the first flakes of snow. The dawn was breaking slowly; as if daylight itself were reluctant to make an appearance. The conditions did nothing to soothe his impatience and sense of ire.

He was annoyed that Clifford had been overhauled and killed with around three hundred valuable men. He was annoyed that the army of York had moved so quickly from south of the River Aire. He was annoyed that the Yorkists had been allowed to gain the wider ridge at the far side of the plateau without contest; and he was also annoyed at how long it was taking his own army to take up its position.

Thanks to the Yorkists securing the far side of the plateau, the forces of Lancaster, vast as they were, had been forced to squeeze into a relatively constrained area south of Towton village, on the lower, and narrower of the two ridges on the plateau. There were tens of thousands of men, from every village, town, and city in England. Perhaps two thirds of the kingdom's nobles had rallied to the Lancastrian cause, and most of them had assembled here with all their strength, intent to finish the menace of the House of York, once and for all.

Sir Andrew Trollope, perhaps the best military mind on the Lancastrian side, had initially been dissatisfied with the position they had been forced to adopt, but he was now busy making his recommendations. His solution was to have only two divisions forward; the vaward and mainward, with the rearward in reserve. This was the only manageable way to cram the entire army into the tight triangle of space before Towton. It would also have the advantage of providing real depth.

When it came to the close-quarter clash of arms, the Lancastrian army would be an immovable block. The Yorkists could push all they wanted, but the solid mass of Lancastrians would be going nowhere. Northumberland would command the vaward on the left, whilst Somerset himself would command the mainward on the right. Exeter would command the rearward.

As he sat upon his charger, brooding, Somerset tried to ignore the clamour of thousands of voices all around him, and instead focused his attention on the horizon. He squinted through the sharp wind and the gloom to study the dark ridgeline almost half a mile away to his front. He could see isolated trees on the higher part of the plateau, and a long dark smear that resembled a distant hedgerow, but as the light gradually intruded on the scene, he began to realise he was looking at the Yorkist line; their banners and standards becoming increasingly clear as the visibility improved.

"There's more of them than I thought." Observed Somerset, sourly.

Trollope, sitting astride his own charger beside the duke, was phlegmatic.

"It seems that way, My Lord, simply because they are stretched out across a wider ridge. There will be no depth to that line."

Somerset gave Trollope a sideways glance.

"It's impossible to tell at this distance. Their strength is anybody's guess."

Trollope was unruffled.

"Study the banners, My Lord. It is difficult to tell in this light, but the banners tell the story. I see York himself, Warwick and Fauconberg. I think there may even be Fitzwalter's up there, amongst the lesser nobles and knights. But there is one banner missing."

Somerset frowned, looked back towards the distant ridge, and squinted even harder into the wind.

"I do not see Norfolk, My Lord." Trollope clarified. "Perhaps full daylight will tell us a different story, but as yet I cannot see either his personal standard or livery banner, and Norfolk commands a large force. If he is not here, then we will most certainly have the advantage in numbers. Believe me, My Lord; that line up on the ridge is not very deep; perhaps six to eight men at most, and half of those will be archers."

Somerset brooded some more.

"I hope you are right, Sir Andrew."

The veteran knight seemed calm and assured.

"Right or no, My Lord; we have the advantage anyway."

"How so?"

Trollope didn't take his eyes off the distant Yorkist battle-line.

"They have to come to us. They have no choice. They have been on the march for weeks. They are the ones seeking the fight. Many of their men are from the south. If they cannot bring us to battle soon they will suffer from mass desertion. Men will start drifting away back to their land, ready for the spring. And besides, they will either starve or freeze to death if they wait any longer. We meanwhile, have the City of York at our back. Many of these lands are owned by the noblemen in our ranks. This is *our* ground. We can sit and wait for as long as we wish, and never suffer any loss of strength. For York, however, time is everything. He must attack."

Somerset mulled over the logic. It did make sense.
"And when he does, we shall catch him in a trap, My Lord." Trollope reassured him.
The experienced knight raised an arm and pointed over into the far distance, away to the right.
"See yonder, My Lord. Just beyond the left of the Yorkist line is a small wood on the edge of the plateau. See how it drops into the valley that runs along to our right here. We must send a force along the valley bottom; lightly armoured and nimble, who can then climb out of the valley and into the wood unseen, and there remain hidden until needed. When York advances, the wood will be in his left rear. At that point, our force can launch an ambuscade. The sudden attack from the flank and rear will cause panic and the Yorkist flank will crumble, caught between our forces in front and rear."

Trollope turned to look directly at Somerset.
"And as with all battles, once the first men begin to run, the others will swiftly follow. The whole Yorkist line will crumble. And then, My Lord... then you can have all the vengeance you wish upon the enemy."

Somerset felt his contempt for the Yorkists well-up, as it often did. Yes, today he would exact revenge on the men who had caused the death of his father just a few years before.
"Then let us be about it, Sir Andrew. Order the archers to start planting their stakes before them, and let us wait for the Yorkist pup to come down here to greet us..."

*

Edward glanced left and right along the full length of his battle-line, which was becoming increasingly indistinct at its furthest reaches due to thickening flurries of snow. The visibility was getting worse, and Edward dared to hope that Fauconberg's clever plan might just work.

The entire army, or at least as much of it as had crossed the River Aire, was now here with him. Warwick had done a superb job in driving the entire army onwards throughout the night and early morning. As soon as they had arrived in Dintingdale, each retinue and company had been deployed from the line of march straight up onto the ridge to assume their allotted position.

The battle-line stretched for almost a mile by Edward's reckoning, with the retinues of his own battle formed over towards the left, and the battle to be commanded by Fauconberg to the right. The split in the battles was impossible to see however, as the entire line was overhung with the standards and banners of every lord and knight who had answered the Yorkist call.

There must have been nearly twenty thousand men lining the ridge. By the standards of the day, it was a huge army, matched only by the equally massive Lancastrian army which appeared to be packed in, twenty deep or more, on the opposite ridge. He could see at a glance that they had the edge on numbers.

Even allowing for the fact that his own line was longer, and even with the thousands of archers taken into account, it was, at its strongest point, barely eight men in depth. That could change soon enough however, if only Norfolk's men would arrive. The young king looked up into the sky which was now white with falling snow. Although the weather aided Fauconberg's plan, the blizzard might also slow Norfolk's march.

They were on their way, he was promised. The word had come from Warwick barely an hour ago that they were crossing the Aire and marching straight for the field. It was partly Edward's own fault of course, that this large additional force was still almost a day's march behind him. He had allowed himself to be drawn forward by the Lancastrians, and he knew in his own mind that his thirst for bloody revenge had forced him on too quickly.

That said, given the set-back at Ferrybridge that had seen the death of Lord Fitzwalter and the injury to Warwick, it had been essential to take aggressive action in order to shore up the morale of his army. He could not afford to show weakness; not now. His only option was to be bold and take the fight to the enemy. And here those enemies were, waiting for him. So now he must fight them, and pray that Norfolk's men could march fast enough.

Edward wheeled his horse about to face the assembly of nobles who had come into the rear centre of his line for their final orders before battle was joined. He scanned the faces now; nothing more than pale blobs peering out from beneath visors and mail hoods. Nevertheless, they were men of noble birth, encased in metal and adorned with the heraldic devices that marked them out as leaders amongst the thousands of dirty, weary men of the common soldiery.

Fauconberg was beside him, resplendent in his quartered blue lions and white crosses upon a red field. Lord Grey was amongst the assembly, his banner sporting the black ragged staff, as were Lords Scrope, Clinton, and Audley. The Bouchier family were well represented, along with knights such as Sir William Herbert and Sir Walter Devereux, and of course Warwick's old favourite, Sir John Conyers. Each of them was here with the men of their lands; their paid retainers and tenants. The lesser knights had brought several dozen fighters apiece; with each of the greater lords mustering several thousand. Almost every fighting age man from England was here; if not on the Yorkist ridge, then on the opposite one amongst the Lancastrian ranks.

Edward knew they had all gambled on him; some through loyalty to his late father and the House of York, others due more to their general hatred of the House of Lancaster. Some of them were probably making a simple gamble on who was likely to be the winning side, and Edward could imagine the conundrum that those nobles would have been faced with. Should they support a sickly, weak-minded king who was danced like a puppet by Somerset and his kin, or should they support an unproven eighteen-year old boy who pretended to the throne? Well... they had made their choice and they were here with him now. He must justify that choice. This was his moment; his one and only chance to prove his worth, here on this field, this day. The young king drew breath.

"My Lords, nobles, and knights. We have marched many miles to be on this field. You know why you are here. You know that my cause is a righteous one, just as you know the wrongs that you and your kin have suffered at the hands of those who now stand before us on this field. Today is a day of reckoning. On this Palm Sunday, God hath granted us an opportunity to strike down our foes and reclaim our birth-rights. God hath given us a chance for justice. Those who stand before us are tainted men. Men who lack honour and grace. Men of greed and ill-will. Today their mischief will come to an end. There can be no parley. The time for talking has passed. Let no man ask or offer quarter this day. Let us end the menace of Lancaster once and for all."

He scanned the half-hidden faces again as he spoke. They stared back at him, eyes hard, faces bleak. These men knew what the day would bring. They had resolved themselves to the bloodbath to come. They knew it was victory or death.
"Though the enemy seem to be great in numbers, we have an advantage. Our advantage is the quality of the men who stand here beside us. And few men on this earth have the quality of our most noble lord and friend, Fauconberg."

The young king gestured to the old warrior sitting before him. "Listen to his words now, and know that they have my approval. Every man must comply with My Lord Fauconberg's instructions; for all our fates depend upon it."
Edward nodded to the man who had devised their battle plan, noting that the larger flakes of snow were beginning to settle upon the old warrior's helmet. It was going to be a long, cold, bleak day.
"Pray tell them, Fauconberg. Pray tell them."

*

Jack, much to his own surprise, couldn't wait for the battle to start. He had gone through every stage of mindset during the long, bitter-cold night, from gut-wrenching fear that almost made him want to cry out loud, to dumb acceptance that his life may nearly be over at the age of just sixteen. Had it not been for his father's presence, he might, at some point in the night, have considered running away; deserting the army in the bleak darkness. But he hadn't of course. How could he? He was here with almost every man and boy from his village, all of whom knew him; knew his family. They were all in this together. He could not leave them.

And now he stood, shivering like a man with the plague, as the snow-storm blew hard from the south across this desolate ridge of moorland. And something had changed within him. For a start, he was so cold that all he wanted to do was to get warm, and if that meant fighting a battle, then so be it; anything to shake of the gnawing cold and feel some blessed warmth in his body once more. But also, there was the strange, horrifying thrill of standing in the battle-line. Even on the march, he had not realised just how many men had been assembled in this great army, but now, looking back over his shoulder, he marvelled.

All around him, spread out for as far as the eye could see, in open formation, were thousands and thousands of archers. Boys and men like him and his father; pulled from every village in England and adorned with the livery badges of their landlords. Twenty paces away, behind the band of archers, stood the main battle-line of dismounted knights and men-at-arms. They stood, grim-faced, resting on their bills, pole-axes, and spears, arranged in a much more tightly-packed formation beneath myriad banners and standards.

Amongst the mass of longbowmen, the captains of the companies moved ceaselessly; generally older men, grizzled, tough, professional soldiers who had marched with the great lords across the length and breadth of England, and in many cases, France too. They checked on their archers, making sure that the bow strings were being kept dry in pouches and that men had stretched-off their cold, aching muscles. Jack's own captain, a fierce looking individual by the name of Thomas Aston, and a veteran of the Calais garrison, paused briefly as he passed by, looking the young man up and down.

"You alright there, lad."
"Aye, Captain." Jack blurted back through lips trembling with cold.
The veteran nodded and gave the younger man a wink.
"You'll warm up soon enough. It's nearly time."
Aston moved on and nodded to Jack's father as he passed by.
"Keep an eye on your lad, Will. Keep him steady."

Even as Captain Aston was speaking, the sound of hoofbeats, muffled by the falling snow, brought the men nearby to a state of sudden alertness. Looking up, Jack saw a party of three riders cantering along the front of the line of archers. One of the riders, wearing an elaborate surcoat over his armour, detached himself from the other two and reined his horse in about thirty paces in front of Jack's company. The other two rode on past, and as they did, he heard them calling out.
"All captains of archers to the Lord Fauconberg! All captains of archers, close in on the Lord Fauconberg immediately!"

As the two riders continued along the front of the line, the captains, as ordered, began to emerge from amongst the ranks of their longbowmen, jogging with urgency toward the lone rider who sat patiently astride his charger at the very front of the line. One by one, they gathered about him, bowing their heads respectfully as they arrived, until after some minutes there must have been over eighty or more captains assembled.

"Is that Lord Fauconberg then?" Jack wondered aloud.
"Aye, lad." Confirmed his father. "They say he is one of the ablest soldiers in all of England. Let's hope they are right, eh?"
Jack could hear Fauconberg talking, but the combination of wind, snow and distance meant that he could not discern the words clearly.
"What's he saying?"
"Orders for the day, I'm reckoning." Will replied to his son. "We'll know what they are soon enough."

A moment later, as if on some unseen signal, the mob of captains suddenly turned away from the great man himself and began running in all directions, back towards their companies. A loud murmur of anticipation seemed to run through the thousands of men stood waiting in the snow and the wind.
"Here we go." Edgar, another bowman standing to Jack's right, murmured.
"Aye." Will agreed. "Looks like the game's afoot."
And with that, Jack's father reached down and dug his fingers into the grass and soil at his feet, pulling a crumbling piece of dirt upwards between thumb and forefinger. He pushed the dirt to his lips and kissed it, closing his eyes at the same time and whispering a short line of prayer.

Jack watched his father with bemusement and noticed that many other members of the company were performing the same ritual. His father opened his eyes and looked at his son.
"Kiss the ground lad. This may be the earth where we are buried this day."
The statement hit Jack like a slap in the face, but then, after a moment of sickening realisation, he imitated his father's actions. By the time he had done so, Aston was back and standing before them.

"Alright, listen carefully. In a moment, we are going to walk forward, keeping our formation. We will draw level with the Lord Fauconberg who is marking our position. When we reach him, we will stop. Understand so far?"

There were nods and grunts of acknowledgement from amongst the company, and Jack glanced over to where the great lord sat upon his horse. He had moved. He had turned his horse away from the battle-line and was walking it away, towards the enemy, who could barely be seen now because of the heavy snow. Jack watched Fauconberg rein his horse in again and turn back towards them. He was perhaps a hundred and fifty paces beyond the archers now; maybe two hundred. Any further and he would have been lost to visibility in the snow.

Aston continued.
"Once level with him we will string-up and, on orders, loose a single volley at the enemy at full range. As soon as we have loosed, we will turn, and then run back a hundred paces, then stop and reform again. Everyone understand?"
Again, there were nods and grunts of acknowledgement. Jack understood what they were to do, but couldn't understand why. Not that it mattered. He was part of the great mass. Orders were orders. His job was to simply follow them."
"Alright then." Aston said, satisfied that his instructions had been assimilated.
The captain of archers drew his sword, turned about and then held it out to his right.
"Stay level with me... Forward."

Hesitantly at first, but then with a spurt, the chequer-board array of archers surged forward. Jack's cold, stiff muscles protested at first, but then the blood began to flow and he picked up speed, glad to be finally moving. He flexed his fingers around his bow-stave, feeling the tendons in his left forearm stretch beneath the protective wooden arm-guard. To left and right of their own company, the neighbouring companies of archers were moving forward too, their captains keeping tight control of the formations as they advanced. The snow was swirling about them with fresh vigour, coming down thick and fast, but step by step, the figure of Lord Fauconberg became more distinct as the mass of archers gained the ground.

As they drew level with Fauconberg, Jack saw that the great lord was barely ten strides away from the left of their company. He had never been so close to a lord of the realm before, and, as Aston ordered the company to halt, Jack threw a sideways glance at the peer, absorbing the brightly coloured detail of his surcoat with its quartered coat of arms. The Lord Fauconberg, having turned his horse once more, sat there motionless, impassive, staring into the distance towards the enemy.

Jack looked back to his front and strained his own eyes. The blizzard, for that is what it was now, made observation difficult, but he could just about see something in the far distance, beyond the whiteout; a large black smear across what he assumed was the far ridge. That, he thought, must be the front rank of the enemy's army.
"String bows!"

Aston's command snapped Jack's attention back to the present. Fumbling with cold fingers, he pulled his bowstring from the pouch on his belt, unwrapping it from the protective cloth he kept it wrapped in, then looped one end around the top end of his bow-stave and allowed it to slide down the shaft as far as it would go. Having done so, he took the other end of the string and looped it over the bottom end of the stave and allowed it to slide into the nock.

Once done, Jack placed the bottom of the stave against his foot, trapping the middle of the stave between his legs. Then, using his whole body-weight, he bent the top end of the stave inwards and slid the top end of the string up again until it was engaged in the top nock. Within a moment, the bow was strung, under tension, and ready for action. He gave the string a slight pull to test the tension and, satisfied, he looked across to his father, who gave him a wink of reassurance.
"Just stay by me, Jack, and listen to the orders. You'll be fine."
"Aye, father."

"One arrow from each man; longest range, full draw!" Fauconberg's voice carried through the blizzard and was taken up by one captain after another.
"Bodkin points. Nock arrows!" Aston's order rang out, suggesting that they were targeting armoured men, rather than horses.

Jack felt a horrible thrill rise within his chest. He had shot arrows at the butts since his childhood, gradually increasing the size of bow and the poundage of tension he could manage as he grew. By all common standards, he was a competent bowman. Today however, would be the first time he had ever shot an arrow at another person. Not that he could really see his target of course. The blizzard was so heavy now that they would be loosing their arrows at a dark smear in the gloomy-whiteness, simply relying on maximum elevation and a following wind to help their arrows find the target. He slid an arrow from his bag and slipped it into place against his bow stave, nocking the rear end on the bow string.

"Draw!" Fauconberg's voice sounded again.
Once more, the order was repeated by dozens of captains along the line of archers. Will dipped his shoulders slightly and then, with every muscle in his body, and especially his chest and shoulders, he drew the string back and brought the bow back up so that he was angled for the maximum elevation possible. The young man held his breath, locking his left arm straight, his right hand holding the bow-string, the goose feathers of the arrow flight hovering by his jaw. Fauconberg had raised his sword high in the air and, standing before Jack's company, Fletcher had done the same. A moment later, the Lord Faunbconberg swept his sword arm down and roared out the final order.

"Loose!"
The word of command was repeated instantly by Aston and his fellow captains. All along the line, swords were swept down, and the unmistakable cracking sound of bow strings being released filled the air, followed by the sinister 'whoosh' as thousands of yard-long ash shafts streaked skyward, stabilised by goose-feathers, and tipped with steel-pointed death. There was no chance now of any other finish to the day than bloody slaughter. The battle had begun.

*

"Are they advancing?"
Somerset squinted into the driving wind and snow which was gathering momentum with each minute.

"Hard to tell." Trollope replied, attempting to shield his eyes from the snow whilst peering into the distance.
"I'm sure I saw them move forward." Exeter, asserted.
Like several other of the Lancastrian nobles, Exeter had walked his horse to the centre to confer with Somerset. He was feeling impatient, and the freezing weather wasn't helping his temper either.
"Aye, me too." Lord Dacre agreed. "There was definite movement. You were right, Sir Andrew. They know they cannot waste time. I believe they are coming to us through the blizzard. We'll see them soon enough."
Somerset and Trollope exchanged a look.
"In which case, gentlemen, it is time to dismount and join your battles. We will all be in the thick of it soon enough. May God keep you safe and grant us victory this day."
"Aye..." Dacre growled. "And may he grant us the head of that Yorkist pup so that it can join his father's on a spike above Micklegate."
Somerset nodded his agreement with the sentiment.
"Indeed. To your positions, My Lords. Let us get this day's business done with expediency."
His fellow peers nodded their farewells, turned their horses, then trotted off into the blizzard to find their men and dismount; ready to lead the fight. This was how it was for the nobility, as much as it was for the common man; fighting on foot, as was the 'English Fashion'. Their ancestors had done the same at Crecy, Poitiers, Agincourt, and dozens of battlefields across England and France. The horses of the nobles and knights would be held just behind the line, ready for use in the event of a pursuit, or should a man of rank need to traverse the battlefield quickly for command and control reasons.

Aside from that, each lord and knight would be stood on his own two feet, shoulder to shoulder with his men at arms and billmen, to fight beside them with poleaxe or sword. Chivalry was a dream of poets. This was reality; the cold, hard, ruthless slog of close-quarter battle.

Somerset watched the nobles depart, then turned to Trollope. "It won't take them too long to cross that draw and come into range. Have the archers string their bows."
"Aye, My Lord. I'll see to it now."

Trollope urged his horse forward, pushing between two companies of billmen from Dacre's retinue, clad in their distinctive blue and yellow livery. He rode forward to where thousands of archers from the various Lancastrian nobles were arrayed, some twenty paces in front of the main line.

Somerset turned to his groom and page who were standing attentively nearby, dressed in his personal livery. His page was holding the long-handled battle-axe that Somerset would begin the fight with. "Be ready to help me dismount. It won't be long now."

*

Mundric was feeling even more miserable than he had been the night before. He was wet to the bone, and his flesh felt as if it had frozen tight. He was hungry, dehydrated, and couldn't stop his teeth from chattering. On top of all that, he was more than a little scared. After arriving on the field in the hours of darkness, Mundric's company had found itself pushed into a cold, wet, patch of ground where they were exposed to the wind and sleet, and where various companies of archers and billmen became hopelessly intermingled.

There were thousands of men, all deploying onto the field in the darkness and trying to find clear ground on which to establish themselves. Predictably it had become rather chaotic, with men sworn to a range of different knights and peers milling around the meagre fires that the vanguard had managed to kindle prior to the arrival of the main force.

Standing and shivering around one of those fires, Mundric and his comrades had thrown worried looks southwards towards the far ridge. Small specks of light showed where the Yorkist forces were assembling for the coming fight. His sense of dread had only increased when some of the more experienced men, veterans of the fight at St Albans in the livery of the Duke of Somerset, had told their tales of the vicious street fighting that had occurred in that town. Mundric didn't like the idea of being involved in close combat of the kind they had described in gruesome detail. Here, he hoped, he could stand well clear of the hand-to-hand fighting and make do with loosing a few arrows in the direction of the enemy.

There were thousands of billmen, men-at-arms, and knights, all with padded jacks, studded brigandines, and plate armour who could do the close-in fighting, he told himself. The archers could stay well removed and simply use their bows where possible.

Now that the day had dawned however, Mundric was feeling less sure of that theory. The weather had worsened, the sleet turning to snow, which was driving hard into the faces of the Lancastrian army. He had briefly seen the dark, indistinct smear across the far ridge which told him the enemy were at hand and ready for battle, before the visibility had worsened. With much shouting and cursing, the company captains had disentangled their men and managed to form them into coherent blocks again, arranging them in the standard chequer-board formation used by archers, some twenty paces or so in front of the main line of billmen and men-at-arms. Things were becoming more organised, and the immediate prospect of battle was becoming more terrifying in Mundric's mind.

"I'm frozen." The young archer grumbled to nobody in particular.
"You and me alike, Mundric." Came a grunt from Grimwald, standing several paces to his left.
The burly veteran blew a large gob of snot from one nostril, which immediately blew back in the wind and splattered over the Percy livery badge that was sewn on the left breast of his jack.
"Not to worry though. I think we'll be busy soon enough."
Mundric's teeth chattered uncontrollably with the cold.
"Will we really fight in this?"
Grimwald screwed his ugly face up in what passed for a thoughtful look.
"Can't see there's any other choice. We're here now, and so are York's men. What army would dare turn its back with its opponent sitting just a few hundred paces away in full array?"
Mundric had hoped for something less fatalistic, and his mood sank even lower.
"Ey-up..." Mundric continued. "Looks like things are getting started..."
Mundric looked up and over his shoulder. A rider on a big war horse and in full plate armour and green livery had ridden forward of

the main line. Mundric had no idea who the man was, but the captains of the archer companies all looked across to him in anticipation.
"The enemy will be advancing soon." The rider called out. "String your bows."
Instantly, the captains relayed the orders amongst the tight throng of archers.
"String-up" Fletcher's voice boomed from somewhere nearby.

The men of the Ainsty began fumbling under caps and in pouches to retrieve their bow strings from where they had been keeping them dry and out of the elements. Mundric's own fingers were so cold and stiff that he could barely get his pouch open. Eventually however, he managed to locate the string and pulled it free.

With every one of his cold muscles protesting, Mundric strung his bow, dropping the loops into the nocks of the bow-stave and testing the great warbow for tension.
"Listen carefully for orders." Fletcher warned the men of his company as he walked amongst them. "Once we have the enemy in sight, we'll need to loose at speed and with accuracy. We'll need to shoot their archers down faster than they can shoot us down. Getting an early advantage is essential, so nock, draw, and loose like you've never done before."

All around Mundric, his fellow bowmen began loosening their arrow bags in preparation for action. Others stretched off their arms and shoulders, or blew into their clenched fingers, flexing them repeatedly to attempt to warm them and get rid of the numbness.

"Make every arrow count." Fletcher lectured them. "With this visibility, we'll probably be engaging them at less than two hundred paces. Even those of you who are blind won't be able to miss them. So, lock those arms out and hold them..."

The captain stopped talking abruptly and came to a standstill, cocking his head to one side. A few of the men in the company looked across at him quizzically, wondering what he was doing. They caught the sudden look of realisation and fear on his face and heard the strange whispering noise somewhere above them.
"Shit..." Fletcher breathed in a voice leaden with doom.
And then it happened.

The arrow-storm came out of nowhere it seemed. Suddenly the strange whispering noise turned into a collective thrumming whoosh, and then thousands of yard-long arrow shafts descended on the Lancastrian army.

"Ugh!" Grimwald grunted in surprise as a bodkin-tipped arrow slammed into his left arm, went right through the muscle, and then entered his ribs, pinning his arm against his body.

Three paces to Mundric's right, a young lad from Bolton took an arrow straight through his throat and simply toppled backwards like a felled tree. All around Mundric, the ground suddenly bristled with arrows embedding themselves in the turf. A shriek of pain made him glance round, whereupon he saw another member of his company howling in shock as his left foot was pinned to the earth by an arrow.

Across the entire Lancastrian army, a corporate wail of anguish and alarm rose as thousands of arrows sliced down out of the blizzard and hit home amongst the packed ranks. It wasn't just the archers who suffered either. The wave of enemy arrows fell over a broad area, with many carrying into the main battle-line behind, taking down billmen and men-at-arms. The loud 'dink-dink' of arrowheads slamming into plate metal would have sounded almost comical if it had not signified something more deadly.

"Return arrows!" The knight on the horse was roaring above the sound of screaming men. "Loose back at the bastards! Take their archers down!"

"Nock arrows!" Fletcher was yelling, stalking between the men of his company.

In a panic now, and trying to ignore the dead and wounded men around him, Mundric reached down to his arrow bag, curled his fingers around a goose-feathered shaft, and drew an arrow free from the container. Fumbling badly, his heart leaping with dread, he nocked the arrow.

"Draw!" Fletcher order. "Maximum range!"

Mundric leant into it and drew the mighty war-bow back, his cold muscles protesting at the effort. He held the bow at tension, back arched with the bow elevated.

"Loose!" Fletcher roared.

Mundric let fly and the arrow streaked skywards, disappearing into the whiteness. The bow string clattered against the wooden brace on his forearm. And he felt the awesome power of the bow as the stave reasserted itself under tension. All about him, the unwounded archers did likewise, and thousands of arrows lifted into the air, disappearing into the blizzard.
"Nock!" Fletcher roared again. "Quickly now! Let's shoot these bastards down first!"
Mundric dropped another of the long ash shafts into place.
"Draw!" Fletcher ordered, and once again Mundric bent into it and drew the bow string back to his ear.
"Loose!"
Once more, a hail of Lancastrian arrows shot skyward with a collective 'whoosh'. The battle was on between the archers from both sides. It was a simple test of arrow power, and the side who could loose the fastest and the most accurately was likely to win the contest, and so the Lancastrian archer captains repeated their orders, over and over again, sending fresh volleys of arrows into the morning sky. Fletcher stalked between the men of his company, ignoring the wounded and dead, snarling out the orders in a steady rhythm.
"Nock... Draw... Loose!"

*

"Back!"
Fauconberg's powerful voice carried on the wind.
The orders were repeated along the line.
"Back!" Aston instructed, waving both arms back up the slope. "At the trot; a hundred paces!"
Fauconberg was already urging his horse back towards the Yorkist line, and the archers in Jack's company needed no further prompting. Having loosed a single volley of arrows, they turned their backs on the enemy and began running back up the slope towards the main line, which was fronted by the angled, sharpened stakes that the Yorkist archers had themselves driven into the open moorland earlier in the morning.

Jack's breathing came in ragged gasps, his lungs protesting at the sharp intake of freezing cold air, and he grimaced as the wind-driven snow blew directly into his face.
"Why are we going back?" He called to his father as they went.
"To avoid the return volleys, son." Will answered. "The Lancastrians will be loosing straight back if they know we're in range."
As he stumbled back up the slope at speed, Jack tried to imagine the effect their arrows might have on their opponents, and what their response might be.
"That'll do. Hold fast there in line with the Lord Fauconberg!" Aston's voice snapped Jack's attention back to what was happening around him. Looking about, Jack saw that Fauconberg had pulled his horse up and turned it about once again. Obediently, the line of archers slowed to a walk and then halted in line with the peer.
"Turn about! Face the enemy again. Spread out and find your space." Aston barked out the instructions as he moved amongst his men, pushing them into place and insisting that they move into their open-order again, maintaining a dispersed formation.
"What now?" Jack wondered aloud.
"We wait, lad." His father replied.
They waited; but not for long.
Even as they were sorting their formation out, an ominous 'whoosh' filled the air, and thousands of anxious faces looked up into the swirling snow. And then the arrows fell. Thousands of ash-shafts, tipped with steel, descended from out of the whiteness and slammed into the earth some forty yards short of the Yorkist archers. Will watched in fascination as the ground suddenly became a feathered forest of ash-shafts.
"They've dropped short..." He gasped aloud.
"Aye lad. That was the idea." His father grinned at him.
As his father spoke, another whoosh sounded in the air and a second volley of arrows came hurtling down from above. This volley too fell short by the same distance. A few moments later, a third volley descended in exactly the same spot. The ground to the front of Jack's company was thick with arrows now, yet not a single man in the Yorkist ranks had been injured. Jack stared at the spectacle incredulously.

"I'm glad we're not standing there anymore." Edgar laughed, a few paces away.

"Why are they falling short?" Jack wondered.

"Winds against 'em." His father explained patiently. "And we've pulled back from where we loosed at them. And they're firing into the blizzard. They think we're in range and they're trying to shoot us down and gain the advantage."

"Let them waste their arrows, eh?" Aston chimed in. "We'll just stand and watch while they do."

The arrows kept coming; the volleys progressively less distinct as the various enemy companies loosed at slightly different tempos. After the first initial showers it just became a constant rain of arrows. They kept falling; one after another, tens of thousands of them; maybe hundreds of thousands. And every single one of them fell short of the Yorkist line.

The archers of the Yorkist lords looked on with a mixture of relief, disbelief, and derision, as the Lancastrian archers spent their arrows uselessly.

"No discipline in their ranks." Aston shook his head at one point and spat contemptuously as he watched the constant shower of arrows descend.

Eventually, the volume of arrows began to reduce and the pace of their falling slackened.

"Forwards!" Fauconberg's voice called through the blizzard. "Forward to the first position!"

"Forward lads!" Aston prompted his men and waved them forwards. Once again, the Yorkist archers began trotting forward towards the lower slope, where half a million Lancastrian arrows provided a useful mark, like some kind of impenetrable goose-feathered hedge.

"Prepare to loose; maximum range." Aston passed the word round to his men. "Space yourselves out; find your room..."

The Yorkist archers shook out into their dispersed formation again, several paces between each man.

"Stand-by, lads. This time we'll be sending repeat volleys. Time to show those buggers how archery is done properly." Aston was grinning at his men now, anticipating what was to come.

Jack peered into the gloomy distance. He could just about see a grey smear across his front at the furthest extent of his vision. That, he assumed, must be the front ranks of the enemy army.

"Nock!" The order came down the line, and thousands of arrows were dropped into place against bow-staves.

"Draw!"

The massed Yorkist archers bent into their bows and drew back, angling their weapons up at the optimum angle.

"Loose!"

Whoosh! A storm of arrows flew skywards, disappearing into the snow and headed for the Lancastrian army. This time however, there was no pause, and the orders of the captains rolled down the line continuously as their men went about their deadly business.

"Nock... Draw... Loose..."

*

Mundric reached down to his arrow bag and found it was empty. He looked down in surprise and saw that all around him, his fellow archers were in a similar position. Fletcher had recovered arrow bags from dead and wounded men and was busy sharing their arrows out amongst the rest of the company, and Mundric gratefully accepted two shafts from his captain. Within seconds however, he had loosed them and once more found himself arrowless.

The young archer lowered his bow-stave, recovering his breath, which fogged in the cold air. His entire upper body was much warmer now, the muscles on fire and glowing from the repetition of loosing over two dozen arrows in rapid succession. His eyes stung badly however, from the snow-flakes that were still being driven into his face by the wind which blew strongly from the south.

"That'll do, lads..." Fletcher's voice was calling. That'll do. I think we have the better of them."

Indeed, to Mundric, it seemed exactly so. Hardly an arrow had come at them in reply. The Lancastrian volleys, it seemed, had completely overwhelmed the Yorkist archers, who were no more than an indistinct blob in the distance; somewhere deep inside the blizzard. The men of Lancaster had clearly won the duel.

"I reckon we've done for them good and proper." Fletcher looked across at Mundric and gave the young man a reassuring wink. "If they still want to fight, they'll have to come across here and do it hand-to-hand; and climb over the bodies of their own archers in the process."
Mundric grinned back at his captain, daring to hope that, against all his initial fears, his part in the battle had been successful and was now likely to be at an end.
"Prepare to fall-back." Fletcher went on. "They'll probably want us to move back behind the men-at-arms now. We'll need to replenish arrows any..."
Fletcher stopped mid-sentence, and Mundric saw the captain's eyes flick upwards into the snow-storm with a look of alarm. Then it happened; just as it had before.

The familiar, dreadful whoosh sounded loud in the air again, and then a storm of deadly arrows fell out of the blizzard and landed amongst the Lancastrian archers and the front ranks of their men-at-arms.
"Holy Mother!" Someone called out as thousands of arrow shafts slammed into bodies and moorland across the length of the Lancastrian line.

Nearby, an arrow glanced off the horse of the knight who had been issuing orders to the company captains, and the animal reared madly. The knight struggled for a moment, and at first Mundric thought he would be unhorsed, but through superb horsemanship he managed to bring the beast back under control and remain in the saddle.

All around Mundric, men fell to the ground, pierced by the long, deadly shafts.
"Shit!" Fletcher cursed.
Barely had he breathed that curse, when another whoosh announced the arrival of yet more arrows. Again, they rained down en masse, impaling more of Mundric's comrades, and even taking down men-at-arms standing some twenty paces to his rear.
"Fuck! We'll be shot to pieces..." Fletcher swore aloud, his face betraying genuine fear.

For Mundric, his captain's consternation was proof enough that something had gone badly wrong.

"Pull back!"

The mounted knight began bellowing the order repeatedly, and slammed down the visor on his helmet as a precaution. His horse remained skittish as yet more arrows continued to slice down from the snow-filled sky, slamming into the lightly protected archers.

"You heard him!" Fletcher yelled. "Back to the main line. Fall back and reform beyond the men-at-arms!"

Mundric, terrified now, and anticipating the dreaded sting of an arrow at any moment, needed no further prompting. He stumbled backwards, towards the main line, where men were ducking and shying away from the rain of arrows. He could already see numerous bodies, bristling with feathered shafts, littering the moorland. As he moved at best speed, he vaguely registered Grimwald's body, flat on the floor, just a couple of paces away. The older man had initially been wounded by a single arrow. Now, his lifeless body sported no less than four shafts, and Mundric marvelled at how he himself had somehow escaped injury thus far.

"Open the ranks! Let the archers through!" Somebody was shouting.

To Mundric, it felt as if he was in a small, enclosed arena of some kind. His range of visibility was limited to perhaps twenty paces or so by the heavy, falling snow, and within those confines, all was chaos. Panic-stricken archers pushed and shoved at the packed ranks of knights and men-at-arms as they fought to move back beyond the range of the enemy volleys, and all the time, those deadly arrows fell relentlessly from above.

The ground was littered with dead and wounded men, and the pure white snow which had begun to lay thick on the ground, was already streaked with red. Mundric felt his heart sink. His stomach suddenly felt heavy with dread. It was going to be a bloody day.

*

"My Lord, Warwick! What brings you to the field?"

Edward reined his horse in before the party of riders that had ascended the ridge in the centre of the Yorkist line. Richard Neville, Earl of

Warwick, sat before his king and master, astride his charger, surrounded by his personal retinue of knights and his standard bearer. The long standard, coloured a bright red and bearing the white ragged staff amongst other heraldic devices, flapped boldly above the group.

"My sovereign, I am come to do my duty. Your orders I have followed, but now I have no further use in Sherburn. Thus, I have come to the field where best I can serve you."
"Norfolk is here?" Edward almost breathed the name, daring to hope.
"Almost, Sire. His men have passed through Milford and are marching to us now in close column. I have left strict instructions with Norfolk's knights and captains. They must march without rest and join us here presently. They come with perhaps five thousand men, My Liege. I dare say their leading companies may well be approaching Sherburn by now."

Edward felt his heart leap with sudden hope.
"And Norfolk himself?"
"Following, Sire. He is ill; some say that he looks to be near death, for he is suffering from a wasting illness. But he comes; slowly behind his men."
Edward nodded. He already knew that Norfolk was seriously ill. That much had been obvious the last time he had met him. That he had pulled himself from his sick bed and forced himself to march with his men through the depths of winter reassured Edward of the noble's loyalty. And of course, five thousand extra men would be a significant boost to Edward's army in the face of such considerable Lancastrian numbers.

"This is welcome news, Warwick; for the battle is already joined. Fauconberg has command of our archers and is doing great execution amongst the enemy's ranks I believe. We are trying to persuade them to come to us. We have the advantage of the higher ridge, and we can thin their numbers if we get them to advance on us."
"Let them come, My Liege. I have scores aplenty to settle with them who sit across that field."

Edward smiled at Warwick's bravado.
"Indeed, Warwick. But remember you carry an injury. The front rank is no place for you today, no matter your courage. I need you alive, Warwick. You must control the reserve here in the centre, what little

we have of it. Be my eyes and ears. Watch what happens on our flanks. Ride the line and make sure it stays whole and solid. And keep your eyes cast southwards for Norfolk's banners."

"At your command, Sire." Warwick bowed his head in acknowledgement.

Edward grimaced into the snow-storm, across Dintingdale and the almost obscured woodlands beyond it.

"How long exactly before Norfolk's men arrive?"

Warwick considered the question for a moment.

"Three hours perhaps, Sire."

It was more of a tenuous suggestion than a confident assertion. Edward mulled the answer over for a few moments.

"We will hold the enemy for three hours and do as much damage to him as we can, but we need Norfolk here to be assured of carrying the day. Send more riders back to Norfolk's men, Warwick. Tell them to march faster..."

*

"This is sheer bloody murder, My Lord. We cannot stand here and just take this!"

Trollope, back behind the main line now, reined in his horse and made the declaration to Somerset, who sat astride his own charger amongst a cluster of nobles.

"We must shoot back at them." Somerset instructed.

"With what, My Lord? Our archers have expended their arrows. It will take an age to bring more forward from the camp, and by that time we will all be shot to pieces. We must advance on the enemy immediately and regain the advantage."

"I thought the plan was to make the enemy come to us?" Declared Lord Dacre.

"They don't need to anymore, My Lord Dacre." Trollope swung his horse round to face the nobleman from the border county of Cumberland. "They have the advantage of the wind, and they have plenty of arrows. They can outshoot us and outrange us. The longer we stand here, the more men we lose."

As if to reinforce the message, another wave of arrows descended from the grim snow-storm and slammed into the packed ranks of the Lancastrian main line. More men fell, several horses reared, and an audible murmur of disquiet rose across the dense mass of men. That murmur would eventually become a collective cry of panic if casualties continued to mount, Trollope realised.
"We must use our superiority in numbers whilst we can. If they won't come to us, and we can't loose arrows back, then we must advance. We must close the line and beat them through brute force."

Somerset looked around the faces of the nobles. Those faces betrayed a mixture of frustration and bemusement. The weather conditions were appalling, and the situation was already confusing enough. How could it be that their own archers had loosed every arrow and achieved every little, whilst now the men of York were able to inflict such a deadly and miserable arrow-storm upon Somerset's army with seeming impunity?

He peered southwards across the plateau and instinctively steadied his horse as a brace of arrows slammed into the ground just a yard away. He could barely see anything but snow. There was a broad smear of darkness across his front in the distant whiteness which he supposed must be the front ranks of the enemy, but trying to see anything other than that was impossible. The Lancastrian army were like blind men being picked off by those with the gift of sight.

A knight from the Duke of Exeter's personal retinue suddenly cried out in pain as an arrow hit him in the back of the leg. The group of nobles looked round together as the injured knight struggled to control his startled horse.
"My Lord..." Trollope pleaded, urging his horse forward so that he could look Somerset in the eye.

The duke returned his gaze, his mind working feverishly as he tried to decide on the best course of action. Trollope's face was set; certain. He had one of the finest military minds in the realm; an acknowledged fact. Somerset knew that he ignored the man's advice at his peril.
"Let us advance, Sire." Trollope pressed. "We can send a force around their flank through the wood as we discussed. But to stand here now is no longer an option."

Somerset made a decision.

"Sir Andrew has the right of it. Let us go to York and put the damned pup to flight. Return to your battles and dismount. We advance on foot. Dacre; lead the left with Northumberland. I'll lead the right. Exeter; bring up the rear division and, when there is space, be prepared to push it into the line."

There were nods amongst the group, and Trollope gave a deep sigh of relief.

"To your battles, gentlemen." Somerset ordered. "Advance on the trumpet signal."

The Assault

It was Palm Sunday, one of the holiest days of the year, and Sim of Dringhouses should have been getting ready for church alongside his wife and two young children. Instead, bill in hand, he was ducking and cringing beneath a constant rain of deadly arrows.

Dringhouses was a small village some two miles south from the city walls of York. Another mile south and he would have lived in the Ainsty, which were Percy lands. Dringhouses however, was owned by the city corporation, and Sim rented a thin strip of land that ran down from the low ridge on which his village sat, towards the common land of the Knaves' Mire.

A lane ran alongside the balk of his field which folk used to access the common land. In fact, people even called the lane after him; Sim's Balk Lane. That made Sim feel important, and he was relatively happy with his lot in life. The land was fertile, the taxes fair, and every Sunday he would attend the village church which was named after the great English confessor king, Edward.

But that peaceful life had been ripped apart recently with the arrival of King Henry, his court, and an entire army. The city corporation had been ordered to raise its militia, and at more than double its normal strength, to fight under King Henry's banner against the usurper Edward, whose father's head now adorned Micklegate Bar. Thus, he now found himself here on this field, wearing a blue and white surcoat adorned with a white rose, over the top of a padded jack, with a deadly billhook in his hand instead of a farmer's hoe. And all around him, men were dying.

The arrows fell relentlessly, like squalls of rain, with monotonous regularity. He had even begun counting the seconds between each wave of arrows. The count was seven. And every time he tried to count eight, the next hail of deadly shafts would fall from within the blizzard and pierce men through. How he hadn't been hit yet he had no idea. All he could do was stand amongst the packed ranks, dip his head after the count of seven, and hold his breath until the latest deluge of arrows had done its deadly business. And then the count would begin again.

All he could think about was that if he somehow managed to survive this battle, he would never leave his village again. His life was simple, and often involved hard toil for a barely adequate recompense,

but it was enough. Enough to live, and enough to have a loving family around him. His current situation however, was like hell on earth.
"Prepare to advance!"
The cry emanated from twenty paces away and was subsequently repeated through the ranks.
"Prepare to advance; on the trumpet call!"

A thrill of fear ran through Sim. An advance? That meant they were going to close with the enemy who waited somewhere out there in the snow-storm. He thought of how bizarre the situation was. He, and all those around him, were men of the City of York, and up ahead, somewhere in the blizzard, waiting to fight him, were the men of the House of York. None of it really made sense to him. Despite that, he was glad to be moving.

He had spent hours standing there in the freezing wind, rain, sleet, and now snow, and for the last few minutes had been pounded by deadly arrows. Going anywhere was better than standing here. Besides, he was six men back in the ranks, nowhere near the front. The front ranks were filled by the captains and veteran soldiers, along with the knights and nobles and their personal retinues of men-at-arms. He and his fellow billmen would do the pushing and provide the weight of numbers. The professional warriors up front would do the real business. Or at least, that's what Sim told himself.

There was a sudden pronounced jostling nearby and Sim glanced to his left. A group of heavily armoured knights accompanied by men-at-arms were pushing their way through the mass of men. Above them flew a colourful heraldic standard.
"Make way!" Somebody was shouting. "Make way for the Lord Dacre! Fill to your right; make way!"

The crowd of heavily armoured men reached the front ranks, ducking momentarily as a new wave of arrows descended upon the Lancastrian ranks. More men went down, whilst the sound of steel points bouncing off plate armour rang out loud amongst the throng. Then, somewhere to Sim's rear, a trumpet sounded a blaring call.
"That's the signal!" A voice called out. "Forwards!"
The trumpet blared out again.
"Forwards! For God and King Henry!"

A ragged cheer went up from amongst the professional warriors surrounding Lord Dacre, and the entire group lurched forwards into the blizzard. Behind them, the men of the City of York militia, Sim included, stumbled after them.

For a brief minute, there was relief from the arrow-storm. As the Lancastrian masses lurched into a steady advance, the Yorkist arrows began to sail overhead on their original trajectory, perhaps hitting a few men at the rear of the press, but otherwise landing harmlessly on vacated ground. For that, at least, Sim was grateful, and despite the difficulty of advancing over the uneven grass tussocks of the moorland, he began to feel a little better as his muscles began to warm.

But then the arrows came again. This time however, they didn't drop from the sky on a steep trajectory. They seemed to whip out of the blizzard from nowhere, directly to the front. Every few steps, more arrows came at them, and men in the front rank went down. Sim stepped over the fallen; some of them already dead, others begging for assistance. After the first two volleys of arrows from the front, the line slowed a little, or so it seemed.

"Keep going!" The voice from the front roared.

The voice belonged, presumed Sim, to Lord Dacre.

"The sooner we close with the bastards the sooner the arrows will stop! Onwards!"

The truth of the statement hit home, and almost instantly the tempo of the advance picked up again. Even as it did so, the blizzard seemed to ease off somewhat; the snow-flakes falling with less density, the wind dropping a little. And then Sim spotted them.

Like a veil being swept aside, the blizzard seemed to disappear in an instant, and Sim finally observed the source of their torment. He caught his breath, and the shocked ripple of voices around him suggested that everybody else had seen it too. The enemy were there before them. Thousands of men, blocking their way like a solid wall, as far as the eye could see from left and right.

Most of them seemed to be men armed with bows, but somewhere behind those ranks he could see numerous banners at full-fly, indicating where the nobles, knights, and men-at-arms of the Yorkist army stood waiting further up the slope. Sim was agog. He had never seen so many people in one place before. With a shock of realisation, he suddenly understood that every single one of them wanted to kill him.

Another wave of arrows hit the advancing Lancastrian line and yet more men crumpled to the floor. With a sense of utter dread, Sim realised that he was now only two men from the front rank. Peering in horrid fascination over the shoulders of the men in front, Sim noticed that something was happening amongst the enemy ranks. It started as a ripple of movement, barely perceptible at first, but then became more pronounced.
"They're running!" Someone shouted.
"They're pulling back!"
"They've turned their backs!"

Indeed, that is exactly what was happening. Sim could see it now. The enemy bowmen had turned their backs and were stumbling clumsily back up the slope. Sim dared to believe that this might be the end of it, that the enemy had given in to fear at the sight of the advancing Lancastrian host. He dared to hope beyond hope that this was the case, and the shouting from the front rank suggested that somebody else believed that to be true too.
"They're running! After them, men! For God and King Henry! Onwards!"

*

"Here they come!"
Jack paused in his retrieval of arrows to look up quickly. When he did, he caught his breath; not easy when his chest was heaving from the exhaustion of constant loosing of arrows at maximum pull.
Nevertheless, the sight he was presented with was enough to stop any man in his tracks. The blizzard had eased off considerably and the wind felt as though it was dropping somewhat. Down in the lower part of the plateau, emerging from the snowy-mist of the winter's morning, as clear as could be, came a huge, seething mass of humanity.

"Holy Mary!" Jack breathed as he took in the spectacle of the entire Lancastrian army appearing before him, less than two hundred paces distant. Amongst the grey-white early morning backdrop, the

enemy army was like a huge, multi-coloured monster; a vast, writhing hotch-potch of blues and yellows, greens, reds, and whites, with countless banners and standards flying above the advancing mass. It was both a wonderful and terrible thing to behold, for that great force of flesh and steel was coming on at an inexorable pace.
"Drop your aim!" Aston's voice came to Jack's ears. "Loose in your own time; choose your targets. Make every arrow count!"

"Come on, Jack..."
The sound of his father's voice snapped the young archer from his private thoughts.
"Gather some of those arrows then get loosing. Now's the time to do as much damage as we can; before we go back."
Jack looked up at his father.
"We'll be going back? When?"
"When they tell us to. But for now, just keep loosing with everything you've got. Finish as many of the bastards as you can before they get close enough to do us any damage!"

Mumbling acknowledgement, Jack reached down and grasped at the shaft of a Lancastrian arrow that was embedded in the turf. Like most of his comrades, he had expended his own supply of arrows some time ago and was now making use of the thousands of spent enemy arrows that were embedded in the lower slopes of the ridge. With trembling fingers, he plucked out four or five shafts and threw them into his arrow bag, then stood upright and prepared to loose again.

He eyed the oncoming horde of enemy, and with each new step, the detail became clearer. He could see the features of men's faces now; or at least the features of those without full-face visors on their helmets. Also clearly visible was the heraldry of the entire English nobility. Lions, griffons, castles, chains, and the Lord knew what else; every possible heraldic device could be seen amongst the multi-coloured masses. Directly to his front, a swathe of enemy footmen with blue and yellow surcoats caught his eye, and Jack decided to send his next arrow straight into that group.

With practised ease, and muscles that were now warm and aching with repeated use, the young man drew an arrow from his bag and laid it against his bow-stave. Absently, he noted the bits of soil and grass clinging to the long steel bodkin point. He drew back, lowered his aim and aligned onto the very centre of the group he had targeted, then let fly the arrow.

The bow string snapped against the wooden brace on his left forearm and the arrow streaked away. He paused for a moment, watching for the fall of the arrow; difficult in the grey light of early morning and the last vestiges of the blizzard. Nevertheless, he managed to track the shot and thought he saw it pass just overhead of the men in the front rank and land somewhere amongst those behind. "Too high..." He chided himself as he reached for another arrow.

Within a heartbeat, the next arrow was laid against his bow-stave. He drew back, lowered his aim, then lowered it a little more. The low ground across which the enemy were now traversing was making the judging of distance quite difficult. He let fly.

Once again, Jack tracked the flight of his arrow as best he could, and this time was rewarded by seeing a man in the front rank suddenly crumple as the arrow hit him in either his upper leg or groin. "That's better..." The young archer murmured to himself, and he reached down for another arrow.

This time, when he laid the arrow against the bow-stave, he noted that the enemy ranks had reached the slope of the ridge on which he and his comrades were positioned. Suddenly, they seemed much closer than before. He could see the mouths of the leaders working as they barked orders and encouragement. He could see the dull gleam of the swords, poleaxes, and billhooks that bristled from within the wall of armoured and liveried men. He could hear the individual shouts and threats of men who were preparing themselves psychologically for the physical clash.

"Onwards! Send the pretender and his lackeys to hell!"

"For God and King Henry!"

"Prepare to move back to the stakes!" Aston's voice called out, firm and strong above the growing clamour of battle.

Jack spotted a group of heavily armoured men amongst the ranks of blue and yellow. Half a dozen men clad in full plate armour, with another dozen or more around them in half-harness and brigandines. Above them flew an ornate heraldic standard which denoted a man of considerable rank. The young longbowman raised his weapon, the arrow nocked and ready. He aligned his bow and paused momentarily. It felt wrong somehow to be aiming at a man of rank, when he himself was nothing more than a peasant from a small village. But then Jack remembered that this was the enemy, and today, of all days, rank was irrelevant. He let fly.

At such short range, no more than a hundred paces, he barely had time to track his shot, but somehow managed to keep his eye on it. At a hundred yards he could not miss, and he watched in fascination, and then disappointment, as the arrow slammed into his intended target. One of the most heavily armoured men halted abruptly as Jack's arrow caught him on the left shoulder, hammering into him with terrible force. The angle however, was all wrong, and the arrow did not penetrate the armour plate; instead glancing off the sloped surface and sailing upwards into the air beyond the armoured man. A moment later, recovering himself, the man lurched forward again.

"Back lads! Back to the stakes! Take some arrows with you!" Jack looked round. His comrades were all reaching down to snatch at more Lancastrian arrows, grabbing handfuls of the shafts from the earth. Others had already done so and were turning away and running back up the slope towards the line of stakes and their own main line of troops.

"Come on, lad!" Will shouted from his spot nearby, as he rammed a half-dozed recovered arrows into his own arrow-bag. "Back up the hill!"

Hurriedly, Jack reached down and grabbed at the nearest arrows he could lay his hands on.

"Back now, Jack. Come on; let's go..." His father urged him.

Jack turned and began running. His father turned and ran alongside him.

"What now, Father?" Gasped the youngster as he stumbled over the snow-capped grass tussocks.

"Just listen to the orders, Jack." Will gasped back at him. "The Captain knows his business. Just listen to the orders. We go back to the stakes and re-form..." His answer tailed off as the older man fought for breath in the cold morning air.

Up ahead, the first of the archers had reached the stakes and were already turning back to face down-slope again. Aston was there, pushing men into place and bellowing instructions.

"Spread out! Find your ground! Wait for the order!"
Lord Fauconberg was there too, astride his horse, yelling out his own orders to the captains.
Aston turned to face back down the slope and made a beckoning gesture towards the last of his men.
"Come on, you lot! Quickly now! Clear the line of sight!"

Jack and Will stumbled into position amongst the line of stakes and turned about, finding their own space to achieve line of sight. Instantly, Jack saw that the Lancastrian horde was still advancing, and its front rank was now crunching its way through the remaining arrow shafts that their own archers had loosed at the very start of the battle. They were just over a hundred yards away, but seemed to have slowed somewhat as they hit the steepest part of the slope.
"Loose at will!" Aston bellowed. "Straight into them. This is your last chance!"
Without any need for further prompting, the Yorkist archers went about their deadly business.

Jack didn't bother to track his arrows anymore. There was no need. The enemy was an unmissable target; a solid wall of colour and steel grinding steadily upslope towards him. He laid one arrow after another against his bow-stave, drew, aimed, and loosed. He didn't stop to even look where the arrows fell, but just went through the cycle over and again, driving one deadly shaft after another towards the enemy, yet still they came on. They were barely seventy-five yards away now.
"Prepare to fall back through the main line!" Aston's voice carried above the collective roar of angry voices that seemed to fill the ridgeline.
"Make space!" Another voice was shouting from somewhere behind Jack. "Make space for the archers to pass through!"
Jack felt a sudden thrill of fear. The enemy were too close. If they charged now, he knew he couldn't escape them.
"Back!" Aston's voice cut through the clamour like a knife. "Back behind the line! Move!"
"Come on, Jack!" He felt his father's hand on his arm.
Jack turned and ran.

His fear increased as he heard a mighty roar from the Lancastrian host behind him. They had seen the Yorkist archers running and, whether they imagined it to be a full retreat or were simply anticipating the inevitable face-to-face clash, they screamed their defiance and frustration at the morning sky, howling out a lust for revenge and blood.

"Get through! Quickly! Come on! Get through there! Get out of the goddamned way!"

Sir John Conyers, standing at the front of his company of men-at-arms, was frantically pushing archers through a narrow gap in the line. On the archers' part, they crammed into the narrow defile, desperate to reach the comparative safety behind the main battle-line.

Jack threw a look over his shoulder and saw that the enemy were barely forty yards away and gaining momentum as they reached the upper slope. They were coming through the line of stakes now.

"Holy Mary! Holy Mary!" Jack blurted to himself.

"Get through, you tardy bastards!" Sir John was shouting.

Suddenly, like water being drawn through a breach in a dam, Jack found himself pulled into the press of men being ushered through the line.

As he was sucked up in the swirl of soldiery, he caught a glimpse of Lord Fauconberg. The nobleman had dismounted his charger, which was being led to the rear through the press, and a foot soldier in blue and white livery was handing his lord a long poleaxe. As he was bundled unceremoniously through the funnel of men-at-arms, Jack heard Fauconberg's powerful voice carry above the noise of the crowd once more.

"Alright, men. Let's send these bastards to the Devil!"

And then, just as suddenly, Jack was spat out beyond the line of footmen. He found himself spilling onto a spacious ridge, where hundreds of archers were milling around, desperately trying to catch their breath and find their comrades.

"Sir John Conyers' company, over here!"

Aston's voice was unmistakable.

"On me! All men of Sir John Conyers', rally on me!"

"Come on, son..."

Jack felt his father's hand on his arm and looked round.

His father was breathing heavily, his face red with exertion.
"Well done, Jack. Close one that, eh?"

Jack let out a short, nervous bark of laughter; relieved to have reached relative safety. Almost immediately after, he jumped involuntarily; startled by the huge, monstrous roar that erupted behind him. It was a noise like he had never heard in his life and would probably never hear again. It was the initial, collective roar, of tens of thousands of men who knew that death was near, and who were bellowing out their mix of defiance, loathing, and fear, in one corporate howl of emotion. The Yorkist and Lancastrian lines had clashed.

Will grabbed hold of Jack's arm even tighter.
Come on, son..." He shouted above the din. "Close on the Captain..."

*

"For God and King Henry! Onwards!"
Despite his lack of commitment to the fight, Sim found himself yelling his support for the war-cry and adding his voice to the swelling wall of sound that was emanating from the huge mass of men, now taking the final steps up the long slope, towards the Yorkist line.

The advance had been horrendous; terrifying. Like all Englishmen, Sim knew the story of how, almost fifty years before, the English archers of another King Henry had brought a much larger French army to disaster, with much slaughter, on a muddy field at a place called Agincourt. Never in his life however, had he expected that he would have to endure the pure hell that was an English arrow-storm for himself.

The advance into the withering volleys of Yorkist arrows had felt like a hailstorm, only a much deadlier one. Thankfully for him, he had been sheltered from the worst of it. As a common man, he was positioned within the ranks, which were fronted by the most heavily armoured men; the lords, knights, and professional men-at-arms of titled retinues. It was they who had absorbed the brunt of the Yorkist volleys and, although many of them had benefited from the protection afforded by their plate armour, plenty of them had fallen victim to the deadly bodkin-tipped shafts. Any area of exposed flesh, be it a throat, mouth, hand, or even a bit of leg that showed between plates, was vulnerable to the lethal missiles that streaked relentlessly down-slope and into the massed Lancastrian ranks.

Sim had been forced to step over three wounded men during the advance. A fourth, standing directly behind him, had gone down after being struck by an arrow that was deflected off the armour of a man at the front. The shaft had slid over the knight's shoulder, whistled past Sim's left ear, and embedded itself in the face of the man behind him. That experience had forced Sim to duck his head lower as he stomped clumsily onwards over the heavy grass tussocks with their dusting of snow, cringing every time the sound of an arrow whispered close by, or clanged off armour plate somewhere up front.

But now that long, terrifying, deadly advance was over, and the moment was almost upon them. The arrows had stopped coming, and the Yorkist archers had been seen to turn their backs and run. At first thought Sim, it might be that the battle was over already and that the enemy knew they could not possibly stand against the mighty force that the nobles of the House of Lancaster had brought to the field. But then he had seen the Yorkist mainline.

The enemy archers had slipped through that line like water through the cracks in the soil after a dry summer. As the archers had worked their way to the rear, the footmen of the Yorkist lords, armed with bills and pikes, had closed ranks again, filling the gaps and forming a solid wall of steel, against which the Lancastrian line must now surely impact.

Peering over the shoulders of the men to his front, Sim studied the men who awaited them and knew that, just like him, most of them simply wanted to live to see another day. Thus, it was now a simple case of kill or be killed. Nobody could run or turn away, for whoever did so first was a dead man. Fate had brought them all here, and now they must fight to decide what fate had in store for them next.

With horrid fascination, Sim noted the blaze of colours along the Yorkist line. Alarmingly, he noted that the group of enemies facing him directly seemed to be dressed in almost identical livery. Arrayed in their blue and white surcoats, the only differentiating factor between them and his own force of militia was the livery badge which they wore upon their left breasts; what appeared to be a fish-hook or something similar. In the centre of that large group stood a score or more of heavily armoured men, and one of them, wielding a great poleaxe, wore an especially ornate heraldic surcoat. Above the group flew several large, square, livery banners. Those banners were quartered, with opposite quarters showing a white cross on a red background, and a blue griffon on a white background. Amongst the livery banners, a long tapering standard of more complex design fluttered.

Even as Sim studied his opponents, a voice filled with contempt sounded from somewhere in the front rank of his own company.

"Those are Fauconberg's colours. One of the stinking Nevilles!"

A moment later, the same voice roared out a final exhortation.

"Death to the traitors of York! Death to the Nevilles! For God and King Henry... Chaaaaarge!"

A mighty explosion of noise erupted from all around Sim as men, seized with the conflicting passions of fear and anger, gave vent to their emotions and lurched forward in a clumsy run over the last few paces of trampled grass. Sim went with them, swept up in the surge, and heard his own mad war-cry joining the thousands of other voices. And then it happened.

It was a noise like he had never heard before; like heaven and earth colliding. The sound of tens of thousands of heavily armed men impacting against each other, screaming for blood. The clash of steel, the sickening thud of metal cutting into flesh, the cries of rage, of fear, of self-pity and of pain. The sound of battle.

Sim stumbled to an abrupt halt as the men in front impacted against the enemy line and the first exchanges of blades and billhooks began. Men stepped back a pace then lurched forwards again, attempting to avoid blows and then counter-strike. Blades were swung rearwards; overhead and horizontally. All the while, the men in the second and third ranks tried to push their spears, pikes and bills over the shoulders of the men in front, desperately trying to get at the enemy without impeding their own comrades.

The first men went down; some silently, but others with soul-wrenching screams of agony. A harsh metallic smell suddenly filled the air; the smell of blood. It was joined a moment later by the odour of punctured bowels. The little remaining snow underneath melted away in an instant; the grass became trampled, and within moments began turning to mud. The first streams of red began flowing amongst the churned-up turf. Time seemed to disappear for Sim, and all coherence in his life faded. His world became a small space where he was pushed and shoved and where he dodged sharp implements and tried to get at an unseen enemy somewhere beyond the men to his front. All the while, the crescendo of battle rose and drowned out his very thoughts. The bloodbath, he realised subconsciously, was only just beginning...

*

Sir John Conyers shoved desperately at the last of the archers as they crammed through the narrow opening in the battle-line. They were a mix of bowmen from his own company of archers under Thomas Aston, and bowmen wearing Warwick's livery. As the last of the archers slipped through the gap, he gestured urgently to the men-at-arms to either side.
"Alright; close-up! Close the gap! Lock in tight and get ready to receive the enemy!"
He flung a look over his shoulder and saw that the enemy were not much further away than about sixty paces. The great mass of men, led by knights and men-at-arms, were pushing their way through the small forest of sharpened stakes that had been planted before the main battle-line, as was common practice. The enemy would be in position to charge at any moment.
Conyers stalked the few paces it took to position himself at the front and centre of his retinue. His own contingent wasn't huge; half a dozen men at arms dressed in his full livery constituted the front rank, supported by fifteen billmen in full livery in the second and third ranks, with another half-dozen spearmen dressed in their own clothing in a fourth rank. His thirty or so archers, under Aston, were now well in the rear. To his left stood the hundreds of men dressed in Fauconberg's livery, and to his right were men belonging to another knight in Warwick's service. Beyond them stood Warwick's own troops; several thousand of them bearing the white ragged-staff badge.

As the snow continued to fall, he heard his personal banner flap in the wind above his head. Here he was again; another battle-line, on another field, standing beside the nobles and banners with whom he was so familiar. But this time it was different.

This time, the numbers were beyond comprehension. Wherever he looked there were men, standards, and banners; tens of thousands of them. The entire landscape was filled with men. This was a battle on a scale that England had never seen before, and Conyers knew that it would also see slaughter like no man present had ever witnessed. There was no avoiding it. And now he watched in gut-churning anticipation as the enemy closed to within forty yards. Any moment now they would charge.

Conyers could see the faces of the men with open helms, and saw the clouds of hot breath rising from the enemy ranks as they forced themselves up the steep slope of the ridge. He could see mouths working as orders and calls of encouragement filled the air.
"For God and King Henry!"
"With Dacre! With Dacre!"

Conyers heard the name and spotted the blue and yellow standard with its red bull emblem. Dacre came from the north country; almost in Scotland. Around his banner was a huge contingent dressed in blue and yellow livery. Beyond them, over to Conyers' forward left, marched a large block of men in the blue and white livery of the City of York militia. The entire country was here on this field.

"Ready yourselves, men." He warned the men-at-arms to either side, flexing his fingers around his pole-axe as he did so. "Any moment now…"

Barely had he uttered the words when a deafening roar erupted from within the Lancastrian ranks. It seemed to gather momentum and force over several moments until it reached a crescendo and filled every fibre of Conyers' being like a living thing. He felt a tremor of fear ripple through his body at the noise, and then the enemy charged.

It was a clumsy charge; uphill, and across rough moorland capped with snow. Nevertheless, it was terrifying. The wave of screaming, armoured men came bounding across the grass tussocks, their weapons raised ready for the first strike.
"Stand firm, men!" Conyers shouted. "For York! For York!"

And then the enemy charge crashed home.

"Yaaargh!"

Conyers roared in defiance as his first opponent struck out at him. A fully armoured night with a green and white plume in his helmet, the enemy made a direct thrust towards Conyers with his two-handed broadsword. Conyers had guessed what the first move would be and was already responding to the thrust. He brought his axe-head up to catch the blade and succeeded in doing so. There was a grating noise as the sword blade slid along the reverse angle of the axe-head, and then Conyers was flicking the sword upwards and away.

Even as the enemy knight fought to regain control over his parried blade, Conyers adjusted his grip on his pole-axe and then brought it slicing down diagonally into the metal plate that protected the gap between his enemy's breast plate and helmet.

The force of the blow sent the knight staggering back a pace, and Conyers immediately recovered his weapon, bringing it to the horizontal, then punched it forward like a spear, so that the top spike jabbed the enemy hard in his upper chest. Already unbalanced, the armoured man went flailing rearwards into the press. What happened to him, Conyers didn't see, because instantly another man in a brigandine and sallet stepped into the gap and brought his bill sweeping down in a wide overhead strike.

Conyers managed to bring his pole-axe up and block the strike, although the impact sent shockwaves along both his arms. Holding the enemy billman's weapon at bay above head height, Conyers took a quick step forward and kicked his opponent hard in an unprotected shin. The man's leg gave way and he fell forwards. Conyers stepped back hurriedly, withdrawing his own weapon and allowing the man's own body weight do the work.

As the enemy billman dropped down heavily onto one knee, the man-at-arms to Conyers' right smashed him over the head with his own war axe. The man fell sideways onto the floor, where he was promptly stamped on and jabbed with the bottom spike of another pole-arm.

In a matter of moments everything had become chaos, as men fought for space to thrust, parry, or swing. Men were jostled from left, right, and behind, whilst desperately fending off enemies to the front.

The noise of battle was immense, visibility through the helmet visor was minimal, and within moments Conyers was gasping for breath. The energy required to fight in full armour was considerable, and every muscle in his body was working at its maximum. It was horrendous, but for Conyers it was also familiar. He had marched with Warwick before and the field of battle was his natural home, so he allowed his years of training to take over and simply immersed himself in the bloody scrap.

Despite the energy-sapping nature of close-combat, he somehow managed to find his voice and continued to shout encouragement to the men around him. Over and over, he screamed the words, whilst his brain relied on muscle-memory and kept him in the brutal slogging match.
"For York! For York!"

*

Henry Montague, captain of a company from the Welsh borders under Lord Audley, watched the approaching wave of men with grim anticipation. This was not his first battle. He and his men were veterans of this long running feud, and fighting was their trade. Even so, the sight that they beheld was no less intimidating. Never before had Montague seen so many armed men in one place. They were beyond number. So many in fact, that he even lost count of the standards and banners.

Standing to his left and right were other men-at-arms in the permanent pay of their Lord. They, like him, wore extensive armour and hefted high-quality weapons. They were not in full harness as the knights and lords were, but nevertheless they were well equipped for the contest. Backing this front rank of professional fighters were the billmen, levied from the villages on Lord Audley's land. They had the privilege, if that was the right way to look at it, of holding the extreme left flank of the Yorkist line.

Montague glanced to his left briefly. A sparse wood of ragged, leafless trees filled this end of the plateau, just before it fell away dramatically into the valley through which a small beck by the name of the River Cock ran. It wasn't the best spot on the battlefield, to be sure. If it went badly, there was nowhere to run to. Today they must fight, and either win… or die.

The sound of trumpets brought his gaze back to the front again. The last of the Yorkist archers were now desperately squeezing through the ranks of the main battle-line, whilst the archers from his own company were sprinting the last few yards to filter around the end of the line, their warm breaths fogging in the cold morning air.

Coming up the slope behind the withdrawing archers, the Lancastrian army appeared from the depths of the blizzard like an army of ghosts. They were massed in a huge block, moving up the slope like an ink stain spreading across parchment. The ridge here was wider than at the opposite side of the field and, as they advanced, more and more Lancastrians began pushing outwards, extending their line, aiming directly for Montague's company.

"Here we go, my lads!" Montague shouted as loudly as possible to the men around him. "Remember; we are the end of the line. There is nobody beyond us. We must stand like a rock in the ocean. We cannot give up this ground today. We are the anchor for the entire army. Fight well; for there is glory for all today!"

He was rewarded by a half-hearted cheer, although most of his men were already too focused on the enemy to worry about his fine words. The Lancastrian line was barely thirty yards away now, pushing their way past the uncountable arrows embedded in the turf, and the wooden stakes driven into the ground by the Yorkist archers to protect against potential cavalry charges.

He studied the banners and standards. Many of the banners belonged to minor knights who were unknown to him, but he recognised the standards of Lords Roos and Beaumont, which were barely a hundred yards apart and closest to this end of the line. The men beneath those standards wore matching livery, and Montague knew that men who were led by their lord in person would fight hard. "Stand-by…" Montague warned his men. "Do not yield an inch to them. Prepare for the charge, and stop them dead…"

Even as the words came out of his mouth, Montague spotted a man in fine armour raise his sword arm and wave it directly towards his company. At the same time, the man in full harness shouted something to those around him, and immediately a collective roar of defiance rose from the Lancastrian ranks. As one, the mass of enemy stumbled into a clumsy run as they pushed themselves up the final part of the slope in double time.

"Here we go... Stand-by..." Montague braced himself for the initial contact, his pole-axe held at the ready.

Crunch!

It is hard to describe the unique sound created when hundreds, indeed thousands of men, smash together in that initial welter of combat, but the shock of impact was immense. Within moments, Montague was fighting off two opponents; the man-at-arms directly to his front who was armed with a heavy bill, and the man behind him, who continually jabbed his long boar-spear over the shoulder of the man to his front, desperate to strike a blow from a distance.

Montague became isolated in his own little world. He vaguely registered the sound of battle around him; the grunts and oaths, the screams, the clang of metal on metal, and of course the sickly chopping sound of blades biting home into flesh and bone. All of that became background noise however. All that mattered was the handful of enemy he could see through the narrow slit in the visor of his helmet.

Having spent most of the night shivering and almost freezing to death in the sub-zero temperatures, Montague now found himself overheating within moments. The sheer energy produced from fighting whilst clad in a heavy brigandine or jack, and an enclosed helm, generated heat very quickly, and within moments he was dripping with sweat; the inside of his helmet filling with steam like a boiling kettle.

He moved instinctively, parrying thrusts and making his own counter thrusts, keeping his feet placed widely to avoid overbalancing or getting pushed over in the rough and tumble of the press. He turned his head frequently, trying to keep oriented to what was happening to his left and right, whilst never for a moment losing focus on his opponent.

"For God and King Henry!" Somebody not far away was calling.

Similar appeals were cried out from amongst the ranks of both sides, and the enemy charge settled down into a steady slogging match along the line of the ridge.

As the first dead and wounded men began to fall into the snow-covered grass, Montague felt the familiar burn in his muscles as he stretched every sinew in his body; desperately trying to stay in the fight and avoid a deadly thrust from an enemy weapon. It was just the start he realised, of what could be a very long, and very bloody day…

*

No man, especially one in full armour, can fight relentlessly for hours on end without opportunities to rest, and even in his prime of youth, Edward, Earl of March and claimant to the crown of England, recognised the need to rest momentarily. The Lancastrians hadn't made any progress against their line, but likewise they were far from spent, and it was clear that the contest was going to last for some time.

After that initial, ferocious clash, men had quickly become tired, the tempo reducing to a more careful, measured slog. Eventually, almost by mutual consent, each side had backed off several paces as fresh men from the rear were fed forward, and the men-at-arms and lords who had fought that initial clash filtered rearwards to remove their helmets or lift their visors and take a breath. Between the two lines, lay a carpet of dead and dying.

Edward, accompanied by his standard bearer and personal retinue, stepped clear of the rear rank of the line and lifted his helmet visor. His handsome face was flushed red and sweat poured down his face. Resting the spike of his battle-axe on the floor, he glanced up, and the first thing he saw was the heraldic standard of Richard Neville Earl of Warwick. The young would-be king blinked several times and wiped the sweat away from his eyes, and this time when he looked, he recognised Warwick himself, reining in his horse and dismounting awkwardly before him.

"My Lord, Warwick?" Edward greeted him. "What news on our reserves? Is Norfolk here?"

Warwick, dismounted now, lowered himself gingerly onto one knee.

"My Liege, it is done."

"Done?"

"Aye, My Liege. Norfolk's men are marching to join us. I have trusted men, my most senior knights, marking the road and driving them on. Norfolk himself is following on behind more slowly. He is most unwell. But his men are coming, My Liege. If we can hold the enemy but for a while, Norfolk's men will be here and victory will be assured."

Edward allowed a smile to play on his features, and he nodded acknowledgement.

"Your word of Norfolk is welcome, My Lord Warwick. But your injury makes the battlefield a dangerous place for you, as I said before. I cannot have you in the frontline of battle, for to do so would be to lose you in an instant, despite your military prowess."

"I will serve you as well I can, My Liege. As you have bade me, I will ride the rear of the line and make sure our men stay strong and sure. I can see that any gaps are filled. I can watch the whole line and warn of any danger. And I can guide in Norfolk's men when they arrive. And now that Fauconberg is at the front with his household, I can command the archers for you."

The young pretender to the throne took a sweeping glance in both directions along the line of battle. His men at arms and billmen were tight-packed and facing the enemy. A dozen paces behind them, in looser formation but standing in their thousands, were his archers; now with little to do other than adding their limited weight to the press when needed. Behind them, he could see the small bands of mounted prickers, riding the line to ensure that no man quit the field without permission. At the furthest end of the line, to the west, a damp mist obscured the furthest part of the fight.

"As ever, Warwick, your service is greatly appreciated. Do as we have agreed. Shore up the line and keep a watch on our flanks..."

Edward paused to accept the offer of a jug of watered wine from a page who had appeared beside him. Gratefully, he took several long gulps of the fluid, before handing it back to the page.

"Above all, Warwick, keep the pressure on Norfolk's men. Send men back in relays to check on them. There can be no pause for them. No let-up in their march. We need them here, Warwick, and we need them soonest. I do not care if you have to make a pact with the Devil and fly them here; just bring Norfolk's men to the field before midday."

Warwick looked up at his master and nodded affirmatively.
"I will, My Liege."
"Good." Edward nodded back. "Then let us all be back about our business. I am back to the fight."
And without another word, the tall young nobleman turned away and began pushing his way forward into the press once more.

*

"Get ready to charge again..."
Sim heard the voice of a nearby captain pass the warning through the ranks.
"Fresh men to the front..."
Much to Sim's consternation, the men directly in front of him turned to face him and pushed past him. As they moved through the press, one of them, bleeding from a wide gash across the lower part of his jaw line muttered something...
"I need a rest. My arms are nearly dead..."

Sim stared at the man's wound in horrified fascination, for the billman himself appeared oblivious to his injury. Nevertheless, the wild, shocked look in the man's eyes told the story of what it had been like in the front rank during that initial charge. Terrifyingly, Sim now found himself in the very front of the line. Looking forwards, he found himself staring at the results of the first half-hour of combat. The churned-up meadow was strewn with bodies and bits of armour and weaponry; a multi-coloured butcher's yard.

Men lay prostrate across the entire ridgeline, bodies twisted at unnatural angles. In places they were piled one atop another. Just beyond that tide of the dead and soon-to-die, a wall of Yorkist soldiers stood ready for another fight. It was the same group of men in blue and white with the fish-hook livery badges. Although he could see the heraldic standard of the enemy lord that his own captains had referred to as Fauconberg, Sim could not see any sign of the great man himself. In fact, many of the heavily armoured men who had been lining the front of the enemy's ranks initially had disappeared. Could they all be dead already? Were they lying amongst the carpet of bodies somewhere?

A ripple of movement ran through the ranks to Sim's left, and he once again heard the now familiar voice of one of their own lords; the Lord Dacre.
"Let me through... We charge again... This time we'll push the bastards right back off that ridge..."
Sim saw the armoured lord and his personal retinue appear in the front of the line, just twenty yards to his left.
"You heard the Lord Dacre..." A captain was shouting nearby. "We charge again. The enemy are worn down and have less men. We have fresh men at the front. This time we'll sweep the bastards away!"
"For God and King Henry!" Dacre roared from his position over on the left, and his personal retinue echoed his war cry.
"Forwards!"

Hesitantly at first, but then with sudden urgency and pushed on from behind, Sim jerked forwards. He stepped awkwardly up the last few yards of the slope, feeling as if his arms and legs didn't belong to him suddenly. As he marched onwards, he saw the men in the Yorkist lines heft their bills into the ready position and steel themselves for the coming clash.

He tried to work out which of the enemy he was likely to come face-to-face with and hoped that he would find his opponent to be a man of slight build and stature; perhaps some clueless artisan pressed into service. As he studied the three or four potential opponents however, he decided that none of them looked anything like that. In fact, all of them looked like tough, hardened, ruthless killers.

As he closed the last ten yards, Sim looked down, not wanting to catch the gaze of the man who would soon try to kill him. Immediately he wished that he hadn't done so. The sight of the men who had already fallen to the heavy blades of bills and pole-axes was truly terrifying. Appalled at the sight of cloven skin and bone, and the red taint that covered the grass and mud completely, Sim looked back up and instantly locked eyes with a man in the Yorkist line.

He was a man of similar age to Sim, with a day or two of stubble around his chin, and shoulders like an ox. From beneath the wide rim of his bowl-shaped helmet, his dark, hard eyes bore into Sim with a look of grim intent.

Somewhere nearby, a trumpet sounded a ragged call, and then Dacre was roaring his defiance again.
"For God and King Henry... Chaaaarge!"
The pressure of dozens of men pushing from behind gave Sim no choice. He stumbled into a run; desperately trying to find his footing between the sprawled bodies on the ground. With no other option, he screamed his incoherent war-cry along with his fellows and hurled himself towards the waiting enemy.
"Chaaaaarge!"

*

"They're coming again! Let me through! Make way!" Fauconberg snarled at the footmen pressing in against the front ranks as he fought to retake his place in the front line. Like all his men and many of the nobles on the field, after the first initial clash of arms he had found himself temporarily exhausted. Both sides, almost burnt out by the ferocity of that first combat had, by unspoken mutual agreement, drawn away from each other slightly to gather themselves. Now however, the Lancastrians were making another charge, and Fauconberg, having checked on matters at the rear and taken a good drink, was itching to be back in the fight.

He was an old hand at this; probably one of the oldest men on the battlefield. Despite that, he knew that today, of all days, it was all or nothing. As a professional soldier, he knew that there were days when you didn't need to fight; days when you could manoeuvre against your enemy, or days when you could simply choose to ignore them. But today wasn't one of them. He and his nephew had staked everything on their loyalty to the family of the Yorkist lords, and today there would be a decision about who would rule this land hereafter. The winner would hold the crown. The losers... Well, they would all be dead.

The Lancastrians' second charge hit home before Fauconberg and his personal retinue could force their way to the front, and in those first few moments of impact, the ageing lord was shoved in all directions as the crowd of armed men welled up against each other and found their fighting space. Pausing for a moment to make sure he could stay on his feet and trying to avoid being knocked over and trampled, Fauconberg summoned every bit of volume he could muster and roared at the crowd around him.

"Let me through! In the name of God, let me through! I am Fauconberg! Let me through!"

The two billmen in front of him, both wearing his livery, heard his demand and glanced momentarily over their shoulders, before squeezing aside. Instantly, the old warrior thrust himself into the space and pushed forward, followed immediately by the knights and men-at-arms of his personal retinue.

Two more strides, and he was almost at the front of the press. All around him was chaos and noise. In many respects, the nobleman was in his element. This had been his life; the profession of war. The screaming, the clash of steel, the roars of anger, the maddened laughter, the trumpets and drums... As overwhelming and intense as it seemed, it was a familiar backdrop; the song of battle.

Despite aching limbs, the veteran soldier felt the energy and excitement flood through his veins, and he knew that men would be watching him; judging him. They would look for his standard and his livery. Common men, nobles and knights, and even the new king himself; they would all be watching to see how Fauconberg made war. He had a duty to show them.

"Let me through! I am Fauconberg!"

Just as he was screaming out the demand one last time, the man before him, a front ranker in a bowl-shaped helmet, suddenly collapsed onto one knee under a chance blow from the heavy chopping blade of a bill. Even as Fauconberg took another step forward, the bill came down again and chopped the man through his shoulder and neck. The injured man, wearing Fauconberg's own livery, made no sound, but simply collapsed face down in the mud.

The nobleman now found himself looking directly at the man's killer; another billman, also wearing a livery tunic of blue and white, emblazoned with a white rose. The enemy billman seemed almost surprised that he had chopped his opponent down. Fauconberg saw the man look up from his victim and met his gaze. The enemy soldier's face carried that familiar shocked look of a man in his first battle, and when he set eyes on Fauconberg and saw his coat-of-arms and full harness of armour, the commoner's eyes went wider still. For a split second they stared at each other; the billman's eyes betraying a look of awe, Fauconberg staring back at him with nothing more than casual contempt. And then they both reacted.

The enemy billman made a clumsy thrust towards Fauconberg, who simply swung his body away with ease and then parried the thrust with his pole-axe. The impact of the two heavy blades meeting sent a judder up the nobleman's arms, but the enemy billman was the least prepared for it. He recoiled in shock at the strength of the counter-blow and staggered slightly in the mud and the blood beneath his feet.

Fauconberg was already following up, thrusting his own weapon forward like a battering ram, due to not having the room to take a swing with it. The enemy billman saw the thrust coming at the last moment and threw his bill across his body at an angle to try and block the thrust. He got there, just, but Fauconberg's heavy weapon smashed into the shaft of the man's bill with extraordinary force; the result of decades of practice and refinement in skill-at-arms. The enemy soldier fell backwards, completely unbalanced, losing his grip on the bill as he went.

The Yorkist lord saw the man fall backwards into the press and hit the floor. Instantly, somebody stepped over him and took his place. The fallen enemy was as good as dead already. Hitting the floor in the middle of the press was a death sentence for sure. He would be trampled and suffocated within the minute.

In an instant, Fauconberg had forgotten the man, and was already hacking at the new enemy before him. This was Fauconberg's business. The battle was joined, and he was in his element. He jabbed his pole-axe forwards again and felt the joy of battle rise within him once more.
"For York! For York!"

*

Sim had never been so terrified in his life. As he quickly learned however, fear was a great motivator. He saw his opposite number grip tightly on the shaft of his own bill, saw his knuckles turn white with the effort, and watched as his lips peeled back to reveal a feral snarl as he stepped forward a half-pace to lunge towards Sim. Unable to avoid the clash and pushed onwards by the press of men behind him, Sim had no choice but to fight or die.

He thrust his own weapon forward, the curve of the hook catching against the blade of his opposite number. They wrestled for a few long seconds, judging each other's strength, and then Sim managed to twist his weapon to one side and threw his opponents blade away. The respite lasted half a second; no more. The Yorkist billman quickly changed his grip and pulled the bill backwards and upwards, then took a full stride forward with his left leg ready to swing the great weapon down like an axe towards Sim.

As Sim began bringing his weapon up to block the strike, the enemy footman slipped. His left foot, instead of finding a firm piece of turf, slid forwards through the slick mix of mud and blood that had developed at the point of combat between the two lines. The Yorkist's face betrayed alarm as he went down on one knee, his legs splayed. As he tried to stabilise himself, he dropped the haft of his bill and dug it into the ground. It was as good as over for him. Losing your footing in the middle of close combat was a mistake that few enemies would allow to pass; even an enemy like Sim, who was nothing more than a farmer pressed into military service.

With a jolt of realisation, Sim saw his brief chance to survive this combat and finish his enemy first. Clumsily, but with as much force as possible, he swung his own bill downwards and the heavy blade clanged into the enemy soldier's helmet. Above the din of battle, Sim heard the man grunt under the impact. Though the blade didn't have sufficient force to cleave its way through the man's helmet, the blow was heavy enough to stun him and left a large dent in the painted metal headdress.

Again, Sim realised that he had bought himself more valuable seconds, and with a desperate snarl he lifted the heavy bill upwards again, changed his grip, then slammed it down again, axe-like this time, on his enemy. The blade slid into the space between the man's neck and shoulder, down the collar of his jack, and this time Sim found himself amazed at the depth to which the heavy blade bit into the man's body, resulting in a sickening chopping sound as it did so.

And then it was over. The enemy billman, so full of anger and fight just moments ago, simply fell face down into the mud at Sim's feet.

For a moment, the amateur soldier simply stared down at his victim in wonder; amazed at how easy it had been to kill the man. For a brief moment, a sense of elation, born of relief, began to flood through him. He could fight after all. Perhaps he might survive this hell in the end?

His thoughts were interrupted almost immediately by an unintelligible roar of defiance which made him look up quickly. Instantly, Sim felt as if his bowels had turned to water. A fully armoured knight stood before him, having stepped into the gap left by Sim's victim. Over his expensive, polished armour, the man wore a surcoat with an elaborate coat-of-arms design; one which Sim had seen earlier in the battle.

With a sense of horror, Sim recalled his own commanders shouting out their recognition of this man during the advance up the slope. Fauconberg. He was facing the Lord Fauconberg; a peer of the realm, an experienced and fully trained soldier, and perhaps one of the most senior enemy commanders. With a rising sense of doom, Sim realised that he was as good as dead.

And then Fauconberg was thrusting forwards with a pole-axe. The Yorkist lord rammed the weapon like a spear, making use of the spiked crest of the weapon. Sim had reacted simultaneously and brought his bill upwards to meet the thrust. The heads of both their blades met with a heavy, metallic clang, and Sim felt the shock-wave run up both of his arms and into his body.
"Holy Mother..." Sim gasped under his breath as he stared at the full-visored face of the enemy nobleman.

Fauconberg, if he had experienced similar shock, didn't betray it. He stepped forward, physically standing on the dead men beneath him, made sure he was stable, and then thrust forward again. Sim made the near fatal mistake of trying to change his grip for a better posture, just as the fresh blow came again with unbelievable speed. He just managed to block the thrust with the haft of his bill, but as Fauconberg's pole-axe slammed forward, Sim realised that this latest blow had been delivered with even more force than the first.

Sim recoiled under the blow, and his fingers spasmed, losing their grip on the weapon. As he staggered rearwards, his own foot slipped in the mud, and then, with mounting terror, he realised that he was falling backwards having completely released his weapon. In the moments it took him to hit the floor, he wondered how it was possible to fall with so many men at his back. Nevertheless, down he went. Sim hit the churned-up earth with a heavy thud and screamed out in panic as he did so, just before the wind was knocked from his lungs by the impact.

A thousand fates ran through his mind in split seconds. He imagined Fauconberg standing over him, finishing him off with his deadly pole-axe; or the stab of a spear or pike. But just as quickly, the terrified footman realised that he was more likely to be crushed underfoot and drowned in the mud. Barely had he hit the floor than several pairs of legs were stepping over him, desperate to get at the enemy. Feet came thumping down all around him, and one landed on his left hand, grinding it into the mud.

Sim screamed out, partly in pain and partly in terror as another passing foot kicked him in the head. The butt end of a bill or spear smashed into his right knee, and as he screamed at the horror of it all, he could hear the war cries and foul oaths of the men around him.
"Bastards!"
"Kill the rebel scum!"
"It's Fauconberg! Get Fauconberg! Kill the traitor!"
"For York! For York!"

The foot lifted from Sim's hand and he yanked it in close to his chest and then forced his body over so that he was on his stomach. He was wallowing in the mud now and he could see every detail of what was around him. He saw a small metal brooch lying in the mud, right next to a severed finger. There were bodies all around him, most of them unrecognisable as humans where they had been pushed further into the mud by the press of men. Somebody stood on his back and he screamed out a protest.
"Get off me! Get off me! I'm not dead!"

The pressure on his back disappeared, and Sim instinctively scrambled forward, his hands grappling for purchase but finding only blood-soaked mud. He pushed himself on between endless pairs of legs and heavy feet, using his own legs to propel himself forward. All the while, he was stepped on and battered by the butt ends of weapons wielded by men who had no eyes for that below their feet, only for the enemy to their front.

After what seemed like an age, there were no more legs, and suddenly he found himself staring at a wide moorland, dusted with snow and littered with bodies. Gasping, covered from head to toe in thick dark mud, Sim rolled onto his left elbow and looked behind him. The press of battle was beyond him now and, much to his relief, the chance of being trampled to death had diminished markedly. He lay there, his chest heaving, drinking in the cold winter air; the horror of the experience subsiding slowly.

Eventually he found the energy to push himself up into a sitting position and looked about him again. At the back of the press, archers moved around the slope, pulling spent arrows from the ground. Wherever they found an undamaged one, they nocked it and fired it high over the press towards the rear ranks of the Yorkist host.

After what seemed like an age, Sim pushed himself groggily to his feet. He stood there swaying for a moment or two, and a feeling of nausea came over him. He retched several times, but nothing more than a few drops of watery gunk came up from his near empty stomach. As the retching subsided, he placed his hands on his upper legs for stability and fought to control his breathing. His whole body was shaking uncontrollably. He was so utterly shocked and exhausted that he barely registered the sound of hooves close by.

"Are you wounded?"
He didn't acknowledge the voice at first, not even registering that he was being spoken to. Something sharp poked him in the arse and he stood bolt upright and staggered in a half circle to look behind him. He found himself staring up at a mounted spearman; well-armed and wearing a red and black livery coat, and an open-faced helmet.

"I said, are you wounded?" The man repeated.
Sim stared up at the mounted man-at-arms for a moment, his mind still disoriented. After a moment, he realised what he was being asked.
"No..." He gasped. "No... I don't think so..."
The rider used his lance to point towards a group of men standing nearby.

"Find yourself a weapon then. And go form up with Captain Fitzsimmons over there. You'll be going back in again soon..."

*

"The bastards are clinging to that ridge like barnacles to a ship!" Dacre growled.
He had pushed his way back through the ranks to the rear of the army after the second charge against the Yorkist line had fizzled out. Both armies had, just like the first pause, drawn back slightly by some unseen agreement to gather their collective breath, ready for the next bout of toe-to-toe violence. The ground between the two armies was a carpet of dead, the mutilated detritus of battle; several thousand men already, sprawled out in a bloody morass of mud and body parts across a frontage of more than half a mile. The pitiful groans and pleas of the wounded and dying filled the air as tens of thousands of combatants gulped in huge breaths of cold air and tried to prepare themselves for yet more horror.

"This time we will break them, My Lord Dacre..."
Trollope, his own armour and surcoat streaked with mud and blood, swung his gaze around the assembled lords who had gathered for an impromptu council.
"They are weary now, as are we; but we also have our reserve battle in hand."
Exeter, looking grim and impatient, made a rumbling noise in his throat.
"Aye; we do, indeed. Let my battle lead the next charge. With ten thousand fresh men, I can break that line clean in half."
"Seven thousand men, perhaps, My Lord. The remainder will be needed elsewhere." Trollope corrected the lord, gently.
"Eh?" Exeter frowned; not understanding.
        Trollope looked to Somerset.
"My Lord Somerset, the plan we discussed before the start of the battle. Now is the time for it."
Somerset, who himself looked near to exhaustion from the close quarter fighting, wrinkled his brow.
"The plan?"

"Aye, My Lord. The ambuscade..."

Trollope turned awkwardly in his armour and pointed away to the right.

"Remember the wood my Lord, right on the edge of the field, just before it drops down into the valley of the River Cock. The Yorkists are almost hard up against its edge. We charge their line once more and pin them; distract them. And while that is happening, My Lord Exeter can send a portion of his force under reliable men down this gulley here to our right and filter along the valley edge and into the wood. With the lines in full contact, the enemy will not notice the movement. Lord Exeter's men can form in the trees and then burst out onto the flank of the enemy line. We demolish their flank, or turn it. Either way, the enemy will begin to crumble."

The gathering of Lancastrian Lords followed Trollope's indication and saw, above the mass of men that stretched away to their right, and just beyond the Yorkist line, the tops of numerous trees.

"There won't be much cover in that wood in the middle of winter..." Exeter observed sceptically.

"But enough, My Lord. Just enough to give a force time to form up and begin the advance on their flank. And remember, the enemy will already be locked in combat with our line. They'll be too busy to notice. But we must move quickly. The day is wearing on, and we must break them before nightfall, and before they have a chance to bring up any reserves."

Somerset decided the matter.

"Sir Andrew is right. We must break them soon. We charge again, and Exeter, you can lead your battle in. But find half a dozen good knights and their retinues to execute Sir Andrew's stratagem. Make sure they are fully informed of the plan. But we must move quickly, whilst we still have the advantage in numbers."

Exeter grunted a reluctant agreement.

"Alright. I'll find the men; decent ones who will do a good job. Now, let's be about it and finish this business…"

*

The ground was difficult; treacherous in fact, especially for the men in full armour, or partially harnessed. Twice already, Sir Richard Tunstall, a knight from King Henry's personal household, had slipped and almost lost his footing. But for a helping hand, he would have gone tumbling down the steep, grassy slope of the plateau and into the waterlogged valley bottom where the River Cock had begun to burst its banks from the incessant rain, sleet and snow of the last few days.

Thankfully, the worst of the terrain was behind him now as he advanced cautiously, his breath coming in ragged gasps, into the edges of the wood. Behind him, hundreds of men-at-arms followed on with their own knights and captains, carefully traversing the slope of the plateau. Above and beyond them, on the crest of the plateau, the battle raged on whilst the large force of Lancastrian troops moved secretly into position.

Now inside the trees, Tunstall paused for a few moments, catching his breath and studying the ground ahead. The wood was probably only a hundred yards deep; perhaps a little more. It was not especially thick, and the time of year made the woodland feel even more bare and open than it might seem in the warmer months. He could see, vaguely, beyond the trees, the mass of men locked in combat on the moorland.

To either side of him, the men of his own company began filtering into the edge of the woodland. They squatted down, keeping as low as possible, gathering themselves for the coming clash. The excitement and fear were palpable amongst the crowd of soldiers.

Tunstall waited there for several minutes, allowing more men to work their way into the woodland, knowing that once the attack was launched they would have only one chance to surprise the enemy. Eventually, the edge of the wood became too crowded, and he gave the signal for his men to advance a little further into the trees to create more space.

He led them forward carefully, at a crouch, then signalled for another halt. The line of men dropped back down onto their knees whilst behind them, in the space vacated, more and more men began filling the woodland having climbed up from the valley.

Eventually, the wood began to swell with the hundreds of soldiers now occupying it, and Tunstall felt sure that the enemy must detect them soon enough. Besides that, he noted that the initial clamour of battle was beginning to wane, and he suspected that if he left it any longer, the two battle lines might disengage. Weighing up the situation, and feeling the tension rising within him, Tunstall decided that they must initiate the ambuscade sooner rather than later. Once again, he gave the signal to advance.

This time, he stood up straight as he moved forward, holding his arms wide to indicate that the troops should keep level with him and form a solid line. As he progressed through the wood, the Lancastrian troops fell into formation and soon they were moving as a loose block, filtering around the trees as they went.

Tunstall could see well beyond the edge of the wood now and was able to orient properly. He had chosen his approach well. The end of the Yorkist line was directly opposite him, about thirty yards from the woodland. A group of enemy archers stood in loose formation just to the rear and side of the battle-line, where the men-at-arms of both armies were slogging it out. Somewhere along that line, Tunstall spotted a banner that he fancied was Lord Audley's.

"This is it." He said in a low voice. "We are exactly where we want to be. We will charge them in a moment and turn their flank completely."

The men around him muttered acknowledgement and their fingers flexed around the hafts of their weapons as they advanced; the sense of anticipation rising.

Just as Tunstall reached the edge of the wood, he saw one of the enemy archers turn and glance in his direction. Instinctively, Tunstall came to a halt, and those around him did likewise. The Yorkist archer looked away, and Tunstall began to let out a quiet sigh of relief. But then the archer looked back. He turned to completely face the wood and stared towards it. To Tunstall, it felt as if the man was looking directly into his eyes.

"Shit…" Tunstall whispered.

And then the archer began shouting.

Immediately, more faces turned in the direction of the wood. The archer was stepping backwards now and pointing towards the trees. Tunstall saw the look of panic on the man's face and realised that they had been rumbled.

"Forwards!" Tunstall roared out suddenly, realising that there were just seconds left before surprise would be lost. "Straight into them; chaaaarge!"

He lurched forward, crashing out of the treeline and into the open, and to either side, his men followed his example. A collective roar erupted from within the trees as hundreds of Lancastrian voices howled their challenge and surged forward onto the flank of the Yorkist line.

As he stumbled forward over the snow-capped grass tufts, Tunstall saw the Yorkist archers falling back in panic. A man-at-arms had appeared amongst their ranks and was desperately trying to rally them into some kind of block, turned at an angle to the main line. There were just moments left to execute this critical master-stroke of the battle, Tunstall realised, and he forced himself on as quickly as he could, and bellowed out his war cry as he did so.
"For God and King Henry! Chaaaarge!"

*

"My Lord, Warwick, what news of Norfolk?" Demanded Edward as he pushed his visor up and gratefully accepted the jug of watered wine from his page. It must have been the fourth or fifth time the king had asked the question of Warwick that morning.
Warwick reined in his horse and dismounted awkwardly. Edward was caked in blood and mud, and his armour appeared to be dented in several places; a clear sign that the young king-to-be had been in the thick of the fighting, intent on winning the crown by dint of stupendous personal bravery.

"Near, My Liege..." Warwick assured him. "His men are near. They have passed through Sherburn. One of my riders has just returned to give me the news. I have sent him back to urge them on at even greater speed. Sir John Howard is leading them. They are bills and bow mainly; the cannon being at the rear with Norfolk himself." Edward drank greedily from the jug and then turned his large, dark, intelligent eyes to Warwick.
"The cannon are of no use today. It's the men we need. How long exactly? Three hours have passed already by some mark..."

Warwick thought carefully for a moment.

"Another hour or two at the most, My Liege; not much more. Maybe sooner now that the snow has eased..."

Edward accepted the assurance with a quiet nod.

"Another hour or two..." He repeated in a murmur, his face grim.

The young warrior's mind was working overtime, Warwick could see. He was thinking what they were all thinking. Could they hold on long enough for Norfolk's men to arrive? The battle had been, even by contemporary standards, brutal in the extreme, and had already gone on for longer than most conflicts. Now it seemed that the Lancastrians would charge again. How many times had they come already today? Three? Four times?

The crest and upper slope of the ridgeline was a carpet of dead and dying men; several thousand of them already. In some places the dead lay in heaps where the fighting had been most fierce. The last Lancastrian charge had seen the enemy surging forwards between these heaps, their leading men staggering over the bodies of the fallen where they lay only one deep. The harsh metallic tang of blood hung heavy in the cold winter air, along with the smell of shit from so many punctured guts.

Warwick glanced behind him to where the archers formed the second line behind the men at arms. Behind the archers, the mounted prickers maintained their patrols up and down the line. The entire mass of men was crammed in along a hundred-yard wide strip of ridgeline, beyond which the ground fell steeply away into Dintingdale, where the bodies of Clifford's men still lay from the night before. If the Lancastrians were able to push them back just another hundred yards, it would all be over. The Yorkist army would collapse as it tumbled down the reverse slope. They had to hold.

Even as Warwick and his young master were silently ruminating on Norfolk's men and their ability to reach the field of battle in time, an almighty roar erupted from one end of the line. Instantly, the eyes of every man looked westwards towards the sudden wave of noise. It was clear that battle was being joined again on the left of the Yorkist line. Then, like a rolling wave, the sound of fighting came reverberating along the line as battle was joined all along the frontage of the Yorkist army.

"Here they come!" A voice shouted from nearby, and the line of men-at-arms and knights closest to Edward began readying themselves for another clash.

"It's Exeter!" Somebody else shouted. "That's Exeter's standard!" Edward looked back towards the centre and right of his main line.

"It seems Lord Exeter is showing his face; giving his fellow peers a rest..."

The heir to the House of York looked dour as he took another slug of watered wine.

"I suppose we had best go and greet him then..."

Even before Edward had finished the sentence, a mounted spearman came thundering along the back of the line from the left flank.

"My Liege! We are ambushed!" The words were tumbling out of the galloper's mouth even before he had reined his horse in.

"What?" Demanded Edward, a dark look spreading across his face. The galloper was in a state of alarm, so much so that he never even considered dismounting from his horse before his lord.

"On the left, My Liege! We are ambushed on the left! The enemy has sent a force from within the wood on the far left; thousands of men! They have hit our left flank and the line is being overwhelmed."

"Enough!" Edward snapped, desperate to prevent the man's words from sowing panic through the centre of the line.

"Ride back to the left; tell them I am coming with all my retinue. Tell them to hold! Go man!"

The rider bowed in the saddle then yanked on his horse's reins and thundered away along the line again. Edward turned directly to Warwick.

"Warwick, hold the centre and the right. Tell Fauconberg; no retreat; no backwards step. Push our archers into the main line to shore it up and keep your eyes peeled for gaps, but whatever happens, hold this line. I will take my retinue to the left and steady the flank."

"Aye, My Liege." Warwick acknowledged.

"My horse!" Edward snapped at a groom. "Get my damned horse over here! Mount up and follow me!"

The latter was shouted to the men-at-arms and knights of his personal retinue.

"We go to the left!"

As Edward's charger was brought forward, a page went down on all fours so that his lord could use him as a mounting block. Edward took hold of the horse's saddle and placed one foot on the page's back, then paused and looked back at Warwick.

"Send another rider to Norfolk's men. Tell them I need them here *now*. Tell them to grow wings if need be, but they must come to this damned battlefield before the hour is done..."

*

Sir John Howard, knight, retainer and cousin of The Duke of Norfolk, was in a grim mood. He had now received no less than four messengers from the Earl of Warwick, the last of which had brought a personal message from Edward, Earl of March, the proclaimed king. The message was unequivocal – *'Come now. The battle is at its crisis point. You are needed now.'*

Howard silently cursed the young Edward for committing to battle before the army was fully assembled, yet at the same time, he knew that with the stakes so high there was no chance of avoiding the clash with such a large Lancastrian army at hand. He realised too, that he and his cousin had already committed themselves to the Yorkist cause. If Edward lost the battle today and was killed, they could expect little or no mercy from Henry's nobles, even if they were not present on the field. The options were stark. It had to be a victory for Edward. This was the only throw of the dice left, and for it to fall in Edward's favour, Howard had to get his cousin's men onto the field as soon as possible.

He pulled his horse over to one side of the road and waved his hand impatiently at the leading captain, signalling that they should continue the march along the muddy, churned up morass that constituted the London-York road.

"Keep going; no slacking! Keep the pace up; we're nearly there."

Howard looked back along the column. Six men wide and disappearing beyond the last bend in the road, probably a mile long or more, the column numbered nearly five thousand; men from every village and town in East Anglia. Norfolk had stripped his own county bare, and that of Suffolk too. Marching north through Rutland, they had pressed more men into service. Half of them were archers, the remainder billmen; bolstered by a core of professional men-at-arms and knights like himself.

The cannon, which had been left by Edward's force at Pontefract for them to collect and escort, had been left with Norfolk and his small contingent of personal retainers. Norfolk himself had recognised that, ill as he was, he was a hinderance to his own men.

"Take them on, Sir John." Norfolk had ordered him. *"Take them on to join the young king. I will follow as best I may with these cannon. They will be of little use today, I fear, but the men will be sore needed. So, march with all haste. Do not stop for rest. You must force the men on until you join the main army."*

Warwick's messengers had confirmed exactly that, and so here they were, trudging through the freezing mud and occasional flurry of snow, knowing that every minute and every step counted.

Howard glanced to his right at the small collection of hovels that sat to one side of the main road amongst a dispersed ash wood. A pricker in Warwick's livery waited at the junction where a small track branched off into the village. The knight watched as the pricker shouted something to the men at the head of the column and pointed with his long spear. Howard kicked his horse's flanks and urged it onwards again until he drew level with the mounted man.
"Where are Warwick and March? Is the field of battle far?" Howard demanded of the mounted spearman.

Again, the pricker indicated with his spear along the York road. "Just over a mile, Sir. Beyond the trees and the small valley. You'll hear the sound of the fighting soon enough."
Howard grunted an acknowledgement.
"What is this place?" He asked, waving an arm towards the ramshackle buildings.
"They call it Barkston, Sir. It is the last village before you reach the field. The next village is where the Lancastrian army was found; a place called Towton."
Howard nodded.
"A mile, you say?"
"Aye, Sir; not much more than that."

Again, Howard nodded, then spurred his horse forwards so that he was level with the leading men in the column again.

He looked down at the men in their blue and tawny livery adorned with white lion badges; their breeches splattered with the mud of the road, faces and hands white with cold. Clouds of steam rose as their hot breath clouded in the cold winter air. They looked tired and grim, which was just how Howard was feeling himself. He wasn't sure how much marching they had left in them. They had been going all day and much of the previous night. They needed to reach the field soon. These men, countrymen from the East Anglian fens, had marched hundreds of miles to be here. They had very little left to give, and what little they had needed to be given on the battlefield.

Howard looked ahead towards the next stand of trees and saw that the road looked as if it was dropping away into lower ground. He cocked his head to one side and listened hard. Above the snorting of his own horse and the squelch and stamp of hundreds of feet in the mud of the road, he fancied he could hear distant cheering. "Onwards!" He shouted down at the trudging foot soldiers. "Not far now, my lads. Onwards..."

*

Montague was worried. In fact, he was terrified. The sudden attack from the edge of the wood had taken him and his companions by surprise. They were the very extreme left company of the Yorkist line. Thirty men at arms, like himself, and around sixty archers, all men who had come with Lord Audley via the battle at Mortimer's Cross. They were veterans who knew their business, and as such has been posted on the flank of the army to anchor it against the edge of the plateau. Just as well, because somehow the enemy had managed to filter a substantial force around their flank, using the hidden slopes of the valley of the River Cock, and now they had exploded like a tidal surge upon the Yorkist left. Had the flank not been held by such experienced men, it would have crumbled instantly.

As things stood, that wasn't far off happening anyway. As their captain, Montague had spotted the danger just in time and managed to wheel his company, and the next one in line, backwards slightly to face the onrush of enemy. At the same time, he had pushed his archers forward onto the left of his men-at-arms, extending the line a little further; just enough to hold that initial charge. But now he had poorly armoured archers with shorts swords, knives, and hatchets, battling against knights and men-at-arms in plate armour, armed with bills, pikes, and long-swords. He and his men were holding on, but only just.

In between defending himself and trying to steady the men around him, Montague had been shouting urgent messages to those behind him to send for help. They needed several hundred extra men here at least, in order to form a block on this very end of the line. He and his men could barely stand more than a few minutes against the vast numbers coming at them from the wood, and every minute saw them falling back another pace.

A billman in a white jack came at him with a mighty roar, and Montague had to use all of his strength and skill to block the man's sweeping blow. His arms shuddering under the impact of blocking the swipe, Montague managed to throw the man's bill off to one side and then reached forward with his own. With an oft-practised movement, he twisted his weapon and dug the hook into the top of the man's jack, just beyond his right shoulder, and gave a huge tug. His opponent was jerked forward, caught off balance, and Montague stepped to one side, allowing the man to come crashing face down at his feet. The captain reversed his weapon with dazzling speed and drove the end spike straight down into the small of the man's back near the base of his spine. At the same time, he lifted a foot and stamped on the man's head, driving his face into the mud, effectively muffling his agonised scream.

Barely had he despatched his enemy when the gap was filled by another, and this time he found himself having to dodge the searching point of a wicked looking pike-head. Bringing his bill up again, he swatted the deadly point away several times, desperately fighting to regain a firm footing. The point kept coming for him however, and Montague felt himself taking a step backwards. He knew he shouldn't be giving ground, but against such intense pressure, it was inevitable. As hardened a fighter as he was, and as desperate as he was, Montague felt the first twinge of uncertainty. He didn't think they could hold, and to have such a thought could be fatal. If he was thinking that, then what about his men? How long before they decided it was hopeless and turned their backs?

"For York, for York!"

The cry intruded on Montague's thoughts as he concentrated on trying to get past the point of the pike-head.

"March is here! It's the king!" Another voice was calling.

"York is come! Rally to the Earl of March!" came another

Montague registered a rising surge of noise; a vast cheer of defiance. It erupted around him like a wave crashing against rocks. At first he wasn't sure what was happening, but then he saw the enemy to his front falter slightly. And then it happened.

From his left, a tall, fully armoured man wearing intricate blue and red livery came crashing into view. Even for a veteran like Montague, the vision of the man was awe-inspiring. The figure in blue and red seemed impervious to the enemy blades as he smashed physically into the mass of enemy soldiers before him, swinging his pole-axe about him with unbelievable speed and savagery. Montague saw two men go down under the vicious onslaught and watched in horrified fascination as a sheet of blood sailed through the air splattering across other men nearby.

The enemy line seemed to collapse before the tall knight, and as he stepped into the gap he had created, more armoured men pushed in beside him, dressed in similar livery. The group of heavy men-at-arms had forced their way into the front of the line, relieving the lightly armed archers, and their impetus seemed unstoppable.

"Rally around the King! For York! For York! March is here!"

As Montague began to register the exact wording of the war cries, a standard came into sight behind the group of armoured men, and at that point his mind suddenly caught up. It was Edward himself, come to the flank. The man who would be king; the tall, driven, heir to the House of York was among them, fighting for his birth-right, for the throne, for revenge; fighting for his own. All about him, Montague's men were shouting out in praise of the would-be king, using his various titles.

"Drive them back! No quarter! Follow me!"

The young nobleman of the House of York was roaring defiance as he swung his deadly pole-axe with ever-increasing frenzy, demolishing any man who came against him. His example sent a bolt of energy through the Yorkist ranks on the left flank and Montague felt the pressure of men behind him, pushing forward as they found their courage again, surging forward to reclaim the lost ground on the left of the line.

Montague's emotions switched suddenly from desperation and fear to exaltation. Edward was here with them, shoulder to shoulder, smashing the enemy asunder like the warrior-king he professed to be. With a jolt, Montague realised that they could win here today. With a leader like Edward, how could they lose?

"For York!" Montague screamed as he side-stepped the pike-head and then stepped forward so that he was beyond its dangerous point.
"For York!"

*

"We nearly had them! They're hanging on by a thread! It was only that bastard Edward himself who stopped the whole flank from collapsing!"
Trollope, in his mud-spattered green livery, pushed up his helmet visor as he addressed Somerset, and fought to control his breathing.
"We've nearly done it. One more push, and we'll send them tumbling back off that ridge and running for the safety of London."
"I hope you're right, Sir Andrew. I thought that their flank would have caved in." Somerset sounded frustrated.
"It almost did. We were so close. Damn that bastard of York! He's everywhere!"

Trollope spat into the mud.
"But see, My Lord Somerset; the centre is weakened. Edward of March is over on the far side of the field. We have the numbers here. Let us charge their centre and right one more time. I'm sure we can break through now. It's our best chance to finish this quickly, whilst March is distracted over by the wood. Dacre has had a chance to rest. Send him back in, over to the left of Fauconberg's banner. We'll go in with him. Exeter can get ready to exploit and pursue."

Somerset's eyes wandered over the battlefield. It was an absolute butcher's yard. In all his days he had never seen a field like this. So many dead and dying. The grass and mud were barely visible, so thickly did the dead lay.

"Night cannot be far off. How long have we been at this now? I lose count of the hours."

"Darkness will be here in a couple of hours, My Lord. We must finish the young pretender before then. We cannot afford to let him survive this day."

Somerset nodded his agreement.

"Then let us get to it. I'll find Dacre. In the name of God, let's finish this business..."

*

Jack was starting to get worried again. After their initial contribution to the battle, the archers had been pulled back behind their men-at-arms, who had then borne the brunt of the close-quarter fighting, whilst the archers were held as a second line to simply provide support where needed.

They had launched occasional arrows over the heads of the fighting men, which had landed in the depths of the rear ranks of the Lancastrian horde, but other than that, there hadn't been much for the archers to do in those first couple of hours.

Now however, the archers had been pushed right up against the men-at-arms to shore-up the line. Casualties had been horrendous. Beyond the mass of fighting men, Jack could see bodies laying thick on the ground. All around the rear of the line, wounded men who had been lucky enough to escape the press lay shivering and bleeding, begging for help.

It was clear that the battle was unrivalled in its level of slaughter. Even the more experienced men, the veterans of other campaigns and battles, were muttering that they had never seen anything like it. The battle had raged for hours already and the Lancastrians had made god-only-knew how many charges. That in itself wasn't usual, said the old hands. Battles normally didn't last this long. Both sides were clearly in it to the bitter end, and Jack found himself praying for either victory or nightfall.

There had been some kind of crisis not long ago. He and his fellow archers had watched with wary eyes as the heir to the House of York had mounted his horse and galloped off over to the left with his personal retinue hard on his heels. He could still see the tapered standard of Edward, Earl of March, flying defiantly over on the left amongst the press. Meanwhile, the Earl of Warwick stalked up and down the line between the archers and the men-at-arms, his eyes darting everywhere, watching every development, alert to any potential crisis in the centre or on the right. A flurry of messengers came back and forth to the animated noble, who looked grim-faced and anxious. Every so often, the noble would gallop to the far right and bring his horse to a halt by a hawthorn tree, then stare into the distance, back down the London road.

"He's looking for Norfolk." Jack's father had told him. "He's marching to our aid with thousands of extra men, but they're worried he won't make it before the battle is decided."

Consequently, Jack found himself looking over his shoulder at regular intervals TOO, hoping to see the promised reinforcements arriving on the field. But, as yet, there was nothing to be seen. And now, things were getting even more desperate.

Slowly, pace by pace, the Yorkist line seemed to be moving backwards. It was almost imperceptible. Nobody was consciously doing it. But, after every Lancastrian charge and round of combat, the line seemed to be closer to the reverse slope than it had been earlier. And the line was becoming skewed. Over on the right, the line seemed to be pretty much where it had started the day, just in front of a prominent hawthorn tree. Over on the left, where there had been some kind of emergency, the line was closer to the edge of the ridge now, although the presence of the Earl of March seemed to have stabilised things over there.

Behind the archers, the prickers rode up and down the line, checking on wounded men and sending those with minor injuries back into the ranks, and using their very presence as a deterrent for anyone who might decide they wanted to leave the field of battle prematurely.

"Here they come again!"

The shout from the front of the press snapped Jack out of his thoughts.

"It's Dacre again..." Somebody was calling out the detail.

Throughout the battle, the captains and other professional soldiers who recognised the livery and banners of the great lords and knights of the realm had maintained a running commentary on whose retinues were facing them. Dacre, Somerset, Exeter, Devon, and many more besides; the names seemed to come in rotation. Commenting on this to his father, Jack had received an explanation.
"They're taking it in turns. Resting their men before sending them back in. They've got so many men they can afford to do that. Meanwhile, our lads are stuck in the line regardless. We'll tire before they do, unless night gets here first and saves us..."
The comment hadn't been very reassuring.

The unmistakable sound of men clashing at close quarters erupted once more from somewhere in front. There were curses and screams, the ring of metal on metal, and the sickening sound of metal cleaving flesh.
"Hold them! Hold them!" Somebody was shouting at the front.
Will, standing to Jack's left, reached out and squeezed his son's arm. "Watch yourself here, lad. Don't get sucked in. Just be ready with your bow if anyone breaks through."

There was a violent tussle going on somewhere to the front, just a handful of people away. A flash of colour caught Jack's eye and he glanced up. Waving above the heads of the struggling men in front was a long, tapering standard, bearing a coat of arms which Jack was becoming all too familiar with; a red bull on a blue and yellow field.
"It *is* Dacre." He muttered to himself quietly.

He had seen the enemy lord and his retinue come against their section of the line several times already today, and now it seemed the nobleman was leading another assault.
"Watch out there!" Somebody warned.
Suddenly, the two men-at-arms directly in front of Jack were swept aside in a welter of blood as if they had been tossed aside by some giant hand. And then he was there; standing in the gap like some muddy, blood-spattered god of war. Lord Dacre of Gisland, resplendent still in his tattered livery surcoat, stepped into the gap, pole-axe in hand; its blade and hammer both dripping with blood and gore.

"Close the goddamned gap!" Somebody behind Jack was screaming.
He heard a rising tide of desperate voices roaring in outrage and fear at what was about to happen. The Lancastrians, led by Lord Dacre, were about to punch a hole right through the Yorkist centre.
"Close the bloody gap!"
The world seemed to stand still for Jack for a moment. Everything seemed to slow down in his mind. He stood there staring at the visored helmet of Lord Dacre as the men around him screamed for somebody to close the gap. Jack felt his hand reach for a goose-feathered arrow. He felt himself dragging it free of his arrow bag and laying it across his bow-stave. All the while, he stood there, staring directly at Dacre, who simply stared back at him.
"Stay back, Jack!" He heard his father's voice.

Then, still in slow motion, he was being shoved aside and his father was stepping towards the enemy lord. His father held his bow-stave in his left hand, but with his right he had drawn the short, cheap sword that he had looted off a dead man earlier in the day.
"Father!"
Jack realised what his father intended and knew that it was doomed to failure, even before it had happened. He watched in stunned horror as his father stepped in front of Dacre and drew his sword arm back, intending to slice it down against the fully armoured man.
"No!" Jack heard himself shouting as his father brought the sword down in a sweeping arc.
His words seemed to echo as Dacre finally moved.

In what seemed like a single, sweeping, almost casual move, Dacre brought his pole-axe up to block Will's assault, holding it firm whilst the short sword simply bounced off the studded shaft and slipped from Will's grip. Dacre then swung the axe blade around in a short, but viciously precise sweep, and slammed it into the spot between Will's neck and his collar bone.
"Father!"
Jack watched in horrified disbelief as his father's body simply fell sideways and down like a felled beast in a slaughterhouse. He watched the body fall to land amongst the other dismembered, bloody corpses that littered the ground.

Somehow, he managed to drag his eyes away from his father's body and look back up at Dacre. The armoured lord took a step forward, adjusting his grip on his weapon as he did so. Working without reason or prompting, Jack brought up his bow stave so that the nocked arrow pointed directly at Dacre.
"Close the gap!"
Jack flexed his chest muscles and arms and drew back the bow string.
"Close the fucking gap!"
Out of nowhere, a horse bowled into Jack and sent him staggering sideways. A pricker from the rear had charged into the gap and was thrusting his spear down at Dacre.
"He's mine!" Screamed Jack as he fought to steady himself.
Even as he stumbled to a halt again, two more men barged past Jack, along the flank of the horse, and threw themselves into the gap in front of Dacre, who was now defending himself from multiple attacks.
"He's mine!" Jack heard himself scream as he stepped forward and tried to get line of sight on the enemy lord again.
A man-at-arms in Fauconberg's livery elbowed Jack in the face as he fought his way forward into the gap.
"Get out of the way you fucking idiot!"
More and more men were appearing, filling the gap that Dacre had opened up; patching the line to stop it from collapsing.
"Hold that fucking line! Push the bastards back!"
Jack looked up and saw the Earl of Warwick was directly behind him on his charger, spittle flying from his mouth as he bellowed out orders. The young archer looked back at the press and saw that the gap had now completely disappeared. Of Dacre, there was no immediate sign, though his standard still flew above the enemy ranks just a few yards away.
"Hold them! Hold them!" Warwick was screaming.
Then, under his breath, Jack heard the noble snarl.
"Where the fuck is Norfolk?"
The sound of fighting in the immediate vicinity had begun to fall away, and subconsciously Jack recognised that the enemy had fallen back again. The pattern had become familiar as the day wore on. The Lancastrians would charge, try to break through, fail, withdraw perhaps twenty or thirty yards to regroup, then charge again. Jack

wasn't bothered however. His mind was now elsewhere. Pushing his way into the press of men again and ignoring their curses, he searched for his father's body.

Finding it quickly enough, he slung his bow over one shoulder and reached down to grab hold of his father under the arms. With an effort, he managed to lift the body slightly, but as he did so, his father's half severed head lolled sickeningly to one side revealing the huge gaping wound that had killed him.

"Oh, shit... blugh..."

Jack dropped his father's body back down and staggered away, retching. He stumbled a few paces, gasping for breath, and stood with his hands on his knees, shivering and shaking from a range of emotions, combined with sheer physical fatigue.

"Alright, Jack?"

He felt a hand on his shoulder and looked up.

Captain Aston was standing beside him. The grizzled captain looked down with compassion on the young archer..

"I'm sorry, lad. I saw what happened. Your dad was a good man."

Jack pushed himself upright, fighting to regain his composure.

"It was Dacre…"

Aston looked at him quizzically.

"It was Dacre." Jack repeated. "He killed him. And now I'm going to kill that bastard Dacre."

Aston gave the young archer a pitying look.

"I'm sure you will, lad. But not just yet. They've pulled back again. It will be a while before they charge again. But when they do, don't be foolish. You can't stand against a fully armoured man toe-to-toe. Let one of our men-at-arms sort the bastard. Maybe you can help yourself to his balls after the battle."

Aston tried a grin of reassurance, but Jack simply reaffirmed his intention.

"The bastard is *mine*. I will kill him and avenge my father."

Aston nodded, realising that he couldn't make the boy see any sense through his grief.

"Alright, lad; alright. Get yourself sorted out. I dare say we'll be needed again soon enough."

And with those words, Aston turned away and began reassembling the surviving archers from his company.

Jack looked back towards the cluster of fighting men in the main line. The enemy, it seemed, had withdrawn once more to draw breath and plan their next charge. He took a few steps forward until he was standing amongst the men-at-arms.
"Did Dacre die?" He demanded of nobody in particular.
"You what, son?" A billman asked, looking back over his shoulder.
"Lord Dacre; was he killed in the last fight?"
The men in the line looked at each other in bemusement. Some searched the ground nearby with their eyes.
"Don't think so."
A voice from several yards away called out.
"Lord Dacre still lives. I can see him beneath his standard over yonder."

Jack tried to push through the line.
"What the fuck are you doing?" Someone grunted.
"Let me through; I must see..."
"Piss off, young 'un. Archers to the back."
"I must see..." Insisted Jack.
"Just fuck off! You're getting in the way!"
A man-at-arms shoved the youngster roughly, back out of the main line.

Jack fumed silently for a few moments and looked about him. His eyes settled on the tree. It was an elder tree; old, gnarled, and devoid of leaves, standing like a stark skeleton on the ridgeline. But it was a substantial tree, with solid limbs, and even though elders were not especially tall trees, anyone sitting in its branches would be able to see across the top of the battle line to where the Lancastrians were reassembling. An idea came to Jack's mind, and without further contemplation, he began walking towards the elder...

*

"We almost had them! We were so close..."
From where he was standing, Sim could here Lord Dacre's words clearly. He, along with a number of others from the City of York

militia and the waifs and strays from a dozen different retinues, had been cobbled together into a large, composite company, and attached to Lord Dacre's division after the first few charges earlier in the day. Casualty rates had been high, especially amongst those who had fought in the front ranks during those early hours.

Now, all across the Lancastrian frontage, the surviving lords and knights were working furiously to reform their line for yet another charge, amalgamating companies and retinues as they saw fit. As fate would have it, Sim had found himself under Lord Dacre, who seemed to be a particularly aggressive commander. In that last charge, they had almost broken through the enemy line, with Dacre leading the way at considerable personal risk. How he had managed to escape from the horde of Yorkists that had descended on him in those brief moments was nobody's business. Dacre however, seemed unphased by the danger he had been in. If anything, he was frustrated that they hadn't been able to push right through the enemy line.

"I could see the fields beyond..." Dacre was lamenting as he pulled his helmet clear of his head. "There was nothing but a handful of archers left beyond that frontline. I'm telling you; one more charge and they will crumble. They have nothing left."

The nobleman was leaning on his pole-axe for support and the sweat was pouring down his face. His hair was slick with sweat and plastered to his skull.

"We'll have a drink, gather ourselves, then go again..." He was lecturing the men around him. "Send word to Somerset. Tell him we must charge again; one more time. The enemy is nearly beaten. We'll have them on the run by nightfall."

"A drink, My Lord..."

A page had appeared at Dacre's elbow with a skin full of watered wine, which the nobleman took gratefully. Raising the skin to his lips he drank greedily and then wiped his mouth.

"Ah... That's better... Tonight, gentlemen, when the Yorkists are beaten and the pretender is dead, we will drink proper wine and make a toast to a glorious victory. One more charge is all it will take. This time we must not stop or falter; just break through and keep going. Then watch the enemy line disintegrate."

Dacre raised the skin again, taking another long drink.

"By all that is holy, this is thirsty work..."
He raised his chin and tilted the skin over to get the last drops from within.
Thwack.

The arrow came from nowhere and hit the Lord of Gisland in his throat, square on. The yard-long arrow-shaft went right through his neck so that the bloody point protruded from the rear. Dacre froze in position momentarily and those around him, Sim included, watched in horrid fascination as the goose feathers on the arrow fluttered in the cold breeze. And then, like a felled tree, Dacre simply toppled backwards and hit the ground, dead.

For a long moment, nothing happened. Everybody just stared at the dead nobleman's body in shock and disbelief. Then, as if on some unseen signal, the first helmet visor slammed down, followed immediately by others.
"Reform!" Somebody shouted urgently. "Form up! Prepare for the charge!"
"Go to Lord Somerset!" Another voice was barking out an order. "Tell him Lord Dacre is slain!"

Sim found himself getting pushed into position behind the men-at-arms. He stared down at the dead body of the Lord Dacre, under whose banners he was now forming. He had almost forgotten about the deadly archers who had opened the battle that morning. Their part had been played long ago, or so he had assumed. Dacre's sudden death was an unwelcome reminder that the Yorkist archers still lurked behind the lines on this battlefield, and that they were still a danger.
"Prepare to advance!"
"We need orders from Lord Somerset..."
"Lord Dacre has ordered another charge."
"Lord Dacre is dead..."
"Silence! The aim has not changed. The enemy must be broken. One more charge will do it. Reform!"

Sim allowed himself to be marshalled by the surviving captains and knights. He was exhausted and past caring. All he wanted now was for the day to be over. All along the slopes of the plateau, other companies and retinues were reforming, ready to go again. Beside him, a motley collection of archers were being pushed into the line. Their own arrows long since expended, the lightly armed longbowmen were being shoved in amongst the billmen and men-at-arms ready for one more charge.

Sim briefly locked eyes with a dishevelled young archer wearing a Percy livery badge on his smock. He was a young man; almost a boy still, and he looked as exhausted and as frightened as Sim felt.

"You an Ainsty man?" He asked the youngster.

The archer nodded.

"Aye. From Appleton village. Near the junction of the Wharfe and the Ouse."

Sim raised an eyebrow.

"Not that far from here then? I'm almost an Ainsty man. From Dringhouses, close to the Archbishop's land."

The archer simply nodded back, his thoughts preoccupied with the coming clash. He looked completely done, Sim thought. He had no more time to dwell on it however, for nearby a trumpet blasted out a ragged call to arms, and was followed by a string orders from the nearest knights and captains.

"Prepare to advance..."

"For God and King Henry..."

"Forwards..."

*

Jack saw him fall. He saw the sudden panic of the men around Dacre as they anticipated the arrival of more arrows. There would be none of course. Jack had done what he swore he would do. His father's killer had presented him with the perfect opportunity to get revenge, and Jack had not missed it. He had used the best of his three remaining arrows, and let it fly with every inch of concentration he could muster. Bizarrely, no sooner had the sense of satisfaction risen within him at achieving a direct hit on the enemy nobleman, than it was gone again; leaving behind nothing more than a sense of emptiness.

His father was dead. His father's killer was now dead. And very soon, he might well be dead too. Jack was no commander, but from his perch in the tree he could see clearly across most of the battlefield. It was an absolute slaughterhouse. The level of death and mutilation on display right across the ridgeline was enough to stun even the most experienced veteran. The two armies had been going at it all day. Thousands of bodies lay strewn across the moorland, and the men who were still standing on both sides looked absolutely exhausted. One of the armies would give way soon, and whenever they did, it would be a grim business. Jack however, was at the point now where he didn't really care anymore. He just wanted the day to be over.

"What the fuck are you doing up there? Picking apples?" Jack looked round at the sound of the voice. A mounted pricker, a captain by the look of him, had ridden up to the tree and was glaring up at him.

"I doubt it. This is a bur-tree." Jack responded insolently, using the slang name for the elder tree.

"That's enough of the cheek, lad." Growled the captain. "You're paid to be an archer, not a fucking jester."

The mounted man gestured with his spear.

"Get out of that fucking tree and get back over to your company. If you can't find them, form up under the Earl of Warwick's banners. Those bastards will be coming again soon enough, and this time it will be the decider for the day. If you fight well, I won't have you whipped for your insolence."

The captain didn't say any more, or even wait for a response. He simply turned his horse away and began riding the line again, shouting instructions to any other man who looked like he was shirking or shrinking away. Jack took another look around. He had nowhere else to go and nothing else to do. Slowly, wearily, he clambered down from the tree and began walking back across towards the battle-line.

*

"Dacre is dead. An arrow in the throat. Killed by some common archer whilst he drank."

The Earl of Northumberland had come into the centre now, to the gathering of senior noblemen on the Lancastrian side. A member of the powerful Percy family who ran the eastern march with Scotland, he was in a foul mood.

"We need to finish these bastards soon. It'll be dark before long. What happened to the ambuscade on the right?"

Exeter grunted a reply.

"It made good headway to start with, but then the pup of York appeared with his retinue and stopped our attack sharp. We pushed them back a fair way and did great slaughter among them, but he stabilised their line, and they're clinging to that ridge like a dog with a bone. That little Yorkist bastard can fight; I'll give him that."

"Then let us attack again." The Earl of Devon interjected. "We still have the numbers. And their line is getting thinner. They can't stand much longer, surely..."

"You are correct, My Lord of Devon." Replied Trollope, his green livery almost unrecognisable now due to the mud and blood that stained it. "Their line is thin indeed. But to break through we must prepare carefully. Rather than try to assault along the whole line, we should form our men into blocks; like battles, but not just three. We form the men into powerful blocks, each led by a lord or senior knight, and then we aim those blocks at the point in the line where there are no standards and where the banners are thinnest...."

Even as he spoke, Trollope saw the bemused look on Northumberland's face.

"That's where their line is weakest. Around the standards and banners, you will find their lords, knights, and men-at-arms. There you will find their retained men, and their better billmen. But between the standards and banners, you will find the peasants. The militia and the pressed men. They have lost so many men that they will have archers in the front to fill the gaps. Those are the weak spots, so we form up our blocks and we punch through their line at those points. We only need to break the line in one place and their whole line will collapse."

The assembled nobles exchanged looks.

"I agree with Sir Andrew." Somerset declared, still keen to follow the advice of the veteran from the Calais garrison.

"And we should bolster the blocks with our own archers too. We need weight of numbers concentrated against the thin points in their line." Northumberland growled something unintelligible, then in a louder voice said "Well, we had better get moving then. Daylight won't last forever and there's more snow coming, I tell you. Let's finish this business and put the lot of the bastards to the sword."

"Aye." Somerset agreed. "Let's be about it. Each of us should form a block. Northumberland and Devon, you look for weak points on the left and advance there. Exeter, head over to the right and form a block there. Trollope and I will form blocks in the centre. Watch out for the standards of Fauconberg and the young pretender himself. Stay clear of them."

The assembled nobles grumbled their understanding and turned to head back towards their retinues.

"On the sound of three trumpet blasts, begin the advance..." Somerset shouted after them. Then, turning back to Trollope, he said. "Come, Sir Andrew. Let us do this thing and settle the matter. This day has gone on too long already..."

*

Warwick felt his injured leg twinge as the arrow slashed past him, just a couple of feet away. The same feeling occurred every time a Lancastrian archer found a spare arrow and launched it in his direction; a natural reaction as his sub-conscious mind remembered the pain generated by the arrow which had caught him in his left leg just twenty-four hours earlier during the confused fight at Ferrybridge.

He was an obvious target of course, sitting high on his horse behind the Yorkist main line, and followed everywhere by his personal standard bearer. It was impossible for the enemy to ignore his presence. Fortunately, in addition to the generally poor marksmanship of the Lancastrian bowmen, and their apparent lack of arrows, Warwick was constantly on the move, which made him a much more difficult target to hit.

He was moving now, having just been to the extreme right flank of the Yorkist line, and was now riding back to the centre. He had found the Yorkist right holding its ground reasonably well, but like the whole line, the men there were getting tired, and the ranks were getting thinner. With a better view than most from his elevated position, Warwick could see the piles of dead that were heaped across the slopes of the ridge, showing where the heaviest fighting had been. In all the years this conflict had been simmering, he had never seen a field like this. Both sides had staked everything they had on this fight. One massive, climactic battle to settle the myriad grudges and disputes that both parties held against the other.

Warwick grimaced as he trotted his charger along the rear of the line. If Norfolk didn't appear soon, it was likely that the Yorkist gamble would fail. He had been promising his king all day that Norfolk's men were imminently arriving, yet still there was no sign of them. The army was nearing exhaustion. They had been fighting all day and, by the look of the weak sunlight that seeped through the grey-white haze, that day was almost done. Another couple of hours and darkness would begin to fall. What then? What if there had been no decisive conclusion to the fighting?

He reined in his horse near the centre of the line. Absently, he noted a young archer clambering down from amongst the branches of an elder tree and walking slowly back into formation with his company. The longbowman looked to be wearing the livery badge of Sir John Conyers, one of his own retainers and an experienced captain.

Switching his gaze, Warwick ran his eyes over the line, noting the banners and looking for spots where casualties had left the line without depth. Even with the archers now pushed right up against the billmen, men-at-arms and knights, the line was looking perilously thin in too many places.

Barely a hundred yards away, downslope, beyond the carpet of dead, the enemy was reforming. They had suffered grievously too, but they had the edge in numbers, and they were forming up into great wedges of men, ready to batter against the weakest parts of the Yorkist line.

Movement to the left caught his eye, and Warwick pulled his gaze back to the Yorkist line. It was Edward. The Earl of March and newly proclaimed king was riding back towards the centre, surrounded by the personal retainers of his household, his standard flying boldly above his retinue.

His party came at a steady pace; a lot less urgently than how they had ridden to the left flank earlier that day. Warwick allowed a flicker of admiration to light up his face. The boy knew his business. Not only could he fight like a lion, but he understood that men were watching his every move. He rode slowly, confidently; calling out encouragement and thanks to the men in the line as he passed them by. For their part, the men cheered him. It was a ragged, loose cheer; but they cheered nonetheless. How could men not cheer such a valiant lord?

The enemy saw it too. They would see him; see his standard. They would know that the new head of the House of York still lived; that he was still on the field; alive, defiant, unruffled. And the enemy would wonder if they could ever push that tall, strong, nobleman and his army off this ridge.

Even as Warwick contemplated the approach of his liege-lord, flakes of snow fluttered down before him. He glanced up at the sky and saw that the vague promise of sunshine had faded as quickly as it had arrived. The sky was becoming leaden again; the breeze picking up. There would be another wave of snow before long he guessed.

"Well met, My Lord of Warwick!"
Edward hailed the mounted noble as he drew nearer.
"My Liege; greetings. How goes the battle on the left flank?"
Edward had pushed the visor of his helmet up.
"All goes well. We had a sharp fight of it for a time, but we held the enemy and now the flank is as stable as it can be. I have left Will Hastings to command the very left of the line. By God, Warwick, you should have seen the man fight! He is a lion, and he saved my life on more than one occasion these last hours. If he survives the day, I shall knight him for his service."

Edward patted his horse's neck and cast an eye across the heads of the men in his battle-line, towards the Lancastrian masses.
"They will charge again soon."
"They will, My Liege, to be sure." Warwick brooded as he stared across the battlefield with his master. "I just hope we can hold them again. Our ranks are getting thinner."
Edward glanced at Warwick.

"We must hold them. We must. There is nowhere to run to, not with this valley at our backs."
"I will have the squires and grooms bring all the horses forward so they are close by, My Liege." Warwick assured the young king-to-be.
"Aye; but they will only see use if we win and need to pursue." Edward noted. "If the enemy rolls us back off this ridge, we are finished, one and all. Rather die in the press than get cut down from behind, running for a horse."

Edward had lowered his voice, making sure that their conversation was not overheard by the common soldiery or their retainers. They had to believe that the day could be won. They must not hear any talk of their leaders contemplating the likelihood of escape in the event of a defeat.
Warwick didn't answer, but simply brooded some more.
A flurry of snow blew across the field again, a sign of the returning blizzard.

"We shall enjoy the snow again before nightfall it seems." Edward commented casually. Then, changing the subject, he said. "I see that treacherous bastard Trollope is here."
"Aye" Warwick growled, hearing the name of the man who had once stood in the Yorkist ranks and then deserted to the enemy the night before the battle at Ludford Bridge. "I can see his banner yonder, My Liege. The serpent still lives."
"Well, if he comes in my direction in this next charge, he will not live much longer." Edward snapped in a cold voice. He would never forgive the man's treachery. "And should God give us victory, I will ride him down and have him put to death; the first among many over there who are long due a reckoning."
"Indeed, My Lord." Warwick agreed.

"Who do they still have over there? I can see Somerset's Banners, and Exeter's..."
Edward scanned the enemy line as the snow came down with renewed vigour.
"Northumberland still stands with them, My Liege; and Devon too. I can still see Dacre's banners, but his standard has been lowered. Hopefully the bastard is dead."
"Hopefully they will *all* be dead soon enough." Edward grunted.

Even after a day of relentless fighting, with the odds against him and the numbers too, the young warrior of the House of York thought only of revenge.

In the distance, a trumpet sounded, and was followed by calls from several others. A faint, ragged cheer floated across the plateau, and the mass of enemy lumbered forwards again.

"Here they come." Edward noted. "Time to dismount. I will join your uncle of Fauconberg in the centre. Let us meet the enemy once more. Let us decide who wins the field this day."

He turned to look at Warwick.

"There will be a decision this day. One way or the..."

He paused, staring at Warwick, who stared back with a perplexed expression.

"My Liege?"

Edward stared not at him, but through him; as if he had seen a ghost.

"Norfolk..."

Warwick scrunched his brow.

"Norfolk, My Liege?"

Edward urged his horse two steps closer to Warwick's charger.

"Norfolk has come..." Edward murmured, almost in disbelief, then raised his gauntleted hand to point over Warwick's shoulder.

Suddenly realising what Edward was saying, Warwick gave a start, spooking his horse. Urgently he wheeled the beast clockwise so he could follow Edward's indication.

"By God and all his angels..." The peer breathed as his eyes focused on the middle distance.

The snow was falling quite heavily again now, but through the makings of the blizzard, down in the low ground, like a long snake, a wide column of men was marching out of the distant trees and across Dintingdale, past the bodies of Clifford's men who had been killed there the evening before. Above those contingents flew the banners of various knights, but more obviously, above the column also flew multiple banners bearing a white lion on a red field. Norfolk's men had come. When all seemed lost, when hope was beginning to fade, as the climax of the battle approached, Norfolk had finally come.

"God be praised." Edward breathed, and Warwick fancied he had never heard the young man sound so honest and grateful in his life.

Suddenly, Edward came alive. The urgency and determination that smouldered within him obvious once more.

"This is it, Warwick. This is the moment. Let us not waste it. I will spread the word amongst the men, but quietly. The enemy must suspect nothing. Let them charge home and we will meet them. We will hold them here. We will keep them busy; pin them. And you will ride to Norfolk's men, Warwick. Go in person and guide them in."

He shot his arm out again, pointing to the forward right of the Yorkist line.

"Bring them in there, Warwick. Hard up against the flank of the enemy. Bring them in on our right and swing them round. Hit the enemy in the flank and turn their line inwards. Bring them hard and fast, Warwick. There is no time for dallying. Get their men-at-arms and bills at the front and bring them straight into contact with the enemy. Speed and shock is the key. We have one chance to win this battle outright. Do you understand, Warwick?"

The light of battle was bright in Edward's eyes once more. He was frothing with the anticipation of what was about to happen.

"I understand, My Liege."

"Good." Edward nodded. "Leave your standard bearer here. Men must not see your standard leave the field. Go quickly and go quietly. I will hold the line here. Go bring them, Warwick. Bring Norfolk's men to us. Go now."

"At your command, My Liege."

Warwick turned his horse away, snapped out a string of orders to his personal retinue, then dug his spurs into his horse's flanks and galloped away.

Edward turned his own horse and paused for a second, watching the Lancastrian line as it advanced clumsily through the blizzard, stepping over the bodies of the dead and dying.

"Dismount! One more stand, my lads! Let us meet the enemy with renewed vigour. The time is at hand to settle this business. Let us be about it. Dismount!"

*

"For God and King Henry!"
The shouts came one after the other now, and the block of men that had been coalescing around the banners of the now dead Lord Dacre was growing even larger. More men were joining the block; men wearing the livery of the Percy family of Northumberland. The great lord himself, along with his personal retainers, had formed up at the very front of the block, beside the remaining retainers of Lord Dacre. The Earl of Wiltshire had also joined the block with his own retinue. At the rear, behind Mundric, more archers were being ushered into the formation by irate captains. Captain Fletcher was amongst them, doing his best to create some semblance of order amongst the chaos. Interspersed amongst the block of men from Northumberland, Cumberland and Wiltshire, were the men of the York militia in their distinctive blue and white smocks.

Fletcher was pushing through the ranks, and Mundric called out to him.
"Captain Fletcher! What are we going to do? What's happening?"
Fletcher paused and searched for the owner of the voice. Spotting Mundric's face, Fletcher shot him a grimace.
"We're going back up to the ridge, lad. Only this time we're going in column. We're going to aim between those two great heaps of dead you can see and punch through their line between those two standards you can see. One of them is York himself, the other is Fauconberg. Both hard men. We're going for the soft bit between the two. When we advance, we'll be marching hard, and there'll be no stopping. We're just going to throw every man we've got at their weakest point until that line snaps clean in half."

His grimace changed to a grin.
"You probably won't need your bow, Mundric, lad. But make sure you've got a good blade in your hand. The armoured men at the front will smash their way through the rebel bastards; we'll just be finishing them off as we march over them."
Mundric nodded and gave a frightened grin in return.
Fletcher moved on.

"Come on now, lads; one last time and the day is ours. Nice and simple. Let the lords and knights smash their way through, then follow hard on their heels and stab anything that gets in your way. Another half hour of work and then you can have all the plunder you want."

"Makes it sound easy, doesn't he?"

Mundric looked round and saw the York militiaman named Sim looking at him. The man, a sturdy farming type by the look of him, looked exhausted; his face drawn and pale.

"We'll see, eh?" Mundric muttered by way of reply.

"Aye." Sim offered without enthusiasm. "Happen we will..."

Somewhere over to their right rear, a trumpet sound; once, twice, thrice. A mighty cheer rose from the block of men formed up some hundred yards away to Mundric's right, and the cheer was taken up by his own block.

"For God and King Henry! Forwards!"

*

Fauconberg was a man of war. In his fifty-six years of life he had spent forty of them in military service, much of it in France, and most latterly with the Calais garrison. He was perhaps one of the most experienced, and oldest of the English lords on the field of battle this day. His experience had shown throughout the long hours of slaughter; from his effective handling of the archers and the goading of the Lancastrian forces to attack, to his personal bravery and ruthless competence in close-quarter fighting. But now his age was also showing. He was nearing exhaustion, and his old bones were aching like they had never ached before. His muscles were beginning to stiffen, his arms and legs feeling like they were made of wood.

In the early stages of the battle, during those first few rounds of combat he had been at his best, using all the skill and dexterity he possessed to defeat one opponent after another. Now however, with his energy spent, his ability to fight with such sophistication was waning. In the last combat, he had barely been able to find the strength to wield his pole-axe. Without the energy to employ any of the fancy techniques he prided himself on, he had simply stood there and repeatedly battered his weapon down against whomever came near him. Fortunately, it seemed the enemy were exhausted too; or incompetent, and that had been enough to ensure his survival this far into the day.

Now, Fauconberg stood in the battle-line, his blue lion and white cross coat of arms splattered in mud, blood, snot, and all manner of human innards. Standing amongst his surviving retainers, and the billmen and archers they had brought with them on this long, bitter campaign, he stared grimly towards the advancing enemy. This would be it, he realised. The final combat.

Having fought to the point of exhaustion, one side or the other must give this time. And he knew that if it was his own side that gave way, that he would be a dead man. He would never be able to move fast enough to reach the horse lines, even though they were less than a hundred yards to the rear. His fatigue, coupled with the blood-lust of an enemy scenting victory would be enough to see to that. He was fine with that to be honest. He had lived his life as soldier and, if need be, he would die as one.

He eyed the banners and standards as the blocks of enemy tramped over the carpet of dead towards the Yorkist line. Northumberland, Devon, Somerset, Exeter, Wiltshire, and many more besides. He knew those men. Most of them were young pups. He had served alongside their fathers once, back when he was loyal to King Henry, before he had been almost impoverished by the failure to recompense him for the expenses he had borne to maintain castles and defences on behalf of the crown. But they were his enemies now. They were the same men who had killed his brother, the Earl of Salisbury. So, now he had two grudges against those men; money *and* blood.

He watched as they came on. The enemy had formed into a number of great blocks of men rather than as a continuous battle-line, or even as three battles as was the convention. He watched them carefully as they manoeuvred around the larger piles of bodies where the fighting had been fiercest. The battlefield was a butcher's yard. Even in France, Fauconberg had never seen anything like this. He doubted any man had seen such slaughter since the days when another King Henry, the fifth of that name, had won his glorious victory at Agincourt.

Fauconberg had been a ten-year-old boy then. He had grown up with those stories and wondered if he would ever go down in legend in a similar way. He may well do today, he realised, but for very different reasons; fighting to the last for a lost cause perhaps.

The enemy came on. They were past the biggest body-piles now and gathering momentum. Fauconberg attempted to flex his solid muscles and found that when he did, everything hurt. He hefted the pole-axe, flexing his gloved fingers around the solid haft, and shrugged his shoulders. The metal plates of his armour grated as he did so. And then he stopped, mid-flex.

Something was wrong. Something didn't look quite right. It took him a moment to realise, but when he did, the revelation hit him like a slap in the face. He had thought the enemy had split into blocks to simply find their way past the great heaps of dead which marked the very first contact point from earlier in the battle. But now they were past that tide of dead bodies, the blocks remained separate. There was no extending into line; no change of direction. He looked to his left first and then his right, and realised that the enemy formations were heading for points on the Yorkist line that lay between himself and Edward's standards and banners. It wasn't accidental he realised; it was deliberate.

"They're avoiding us!" He barked out loud.

"My Lord?" One of his nearby retainers asked, puzzled.

"They're avoiding us deliberately!" Fauconberg repeated. "They mean to avoid the strongest parts of our line. See how they aim for the points where are banners are thinnest. They know that there are few knights or men-at-arms there. They are heading for our weak spots with all their strength. They mean to break the line!"

His retainers could see it too now. They could clearly see that none of the enemy was coming near them. Instead, they intended to punch through the Yorkist line on either side. Fauconberg was already picturing what would happen. The lines would break, the Lancastrians would pour through on either side, and he and his retainers would be cut-off and surrounded. And there they would die, together, in a tight circle.

Fauconberg looked along the front of the Yorkist line and saw that Edward had realised the same. The young king's standard was already moving. There was a ripple in the ranks as Edward and his retainers pushed their way along the frontage of the Yorkist line, so that they might be placed to meet the oncoming block of Lancastrians. Fauconberg realised what he must do, instantly. Edward would move to meet the attack of one enemy block, and so Fauconberg must move to meet the nearest of the other enemy formations.

"To the left! My retinue, Fauconberg's retinue, follow me! To the left, quickly now!"

Rather than push through the ranks, Fauconberg stepped out of the line and began moving along its frontage. He moved as fast as his stiff legs would allow him, slipping in the blood-soaked mud. Snow was falling again, like a white shroud descending from the heavens onto the damned. The enemy were less than fifty yards from connecting with the Yorkist line now, and Fauconberg forced himself on, his leg muscles screaming in protest at the exertion. With his helmet visor down, his hot breath created a humid environment within its metal confines, and the aged warrior could hear the blood pumping in his ears. Behind him, he heard the splatter and thud of footfalls as his retainers tottered after him.

"With me! Fauconberg is here! Follow me!" He attempted to shout, although his words came out more as a gasp than a roar.
And with every moment, the Lancastrians took another step closer to victory.

*

"Form-up to the right! Quickly now! Form-up! Bills to the front!"

Howard bellowed the commands at the hundreds of men who were hurrying now from the line of march to assemble into a wide battle-line along the edge of the London to York road. Beside him, The Earl of Warwick chivvied him on in turn.

"Hurry Sir John; it sounds as if the enemy has charged again. We must attack now. There is no time to delay."

Howard turned his head to acknowledge Warwick.

"Two minutes, My Lord, that is all. Let me form the men and then we shall advance. We will hit the enemy with maximum force."

They were sitting astride their horses on the road which skirted along the lower slopes of the plateau towards Towton village. The plateau on which the battle was being fought rose steeply up from the road. There were bodies lying on the very upper slopes, although there was no sign of the actual fighting from their position. The sound of battle was clear enough however. It could not be mistaken; the sound of tens of thousands of men locked in deadly combat.

The faint outline of a narrow track ran up the hill, visible through the layer of snow. It followed the path of a wide, shallow gulley that would allow a slightly less acute climb up onto the plateau. "Advance directly up here, Sir John." Warwick encouraged Norfolk's appointed commander. As soon as you crest the rise, you will see the enemy. You will be directly on their flank. Drive hard into them and do not stop. Roll them up, Sir John; drive them back across the moor."
"Aye, My Lord; at your command..."
"Go now, Sir John. Go now."

Howard turned to look back along the column which was still flooding across Dintingdale and deploying into battle formation. He spotted a man in half-harness on a grey horse.
"Captain Hobbes; Keep pushing the men forward. Billmen first, with the men-at-arms. Archers to the rear. Keep pushing them up the hill. Understand?"
"Aye, Sir John." The captain raised a hand in salute and acknowledgement.
Satisfied, Howard turned to the nine mounted men-at-arms of his retinue who waited nearby, including his banner bearer.
"Dismount, lads, and over to the front with me. We have marched a long way. Now it is time to fight."

Howard swung his leg from over his horse's back and dropped down heavily onto the road. As he did so, a groom urged his pony forward and took the reins of Howard's charger. Having secured his master's mount he then handed down a medium length axe, which Howard took without comment.
"Right. Let us be about it." Howard declared as his retainers assembled around him, drawing their broadswords and adjusting their armour.

"Tell My Lord, Edward, that we are coming, Sir." Howard said, glancing up at Warwick.
"I will, Sir John. May God go with you and give us victory."
"Amen." Howard replied.
   "And Sir John..." Warwick added. "Remember... Give them no quarter. That is the King's order of the day."
Howard nodded his understanding.
"No quarter."
He turned away and began striding along the front of the ever-growing formation of billmen.
"With me, my lads. Let's go and have ourselves a battle..."

*

   "Yaaargh!"
Fauconberg let out a scream that was part rage, part desperation, and part pain, as he rammed the spiked end of his pole-axe at the enemy man-at-arms.
   He was side on to the man, having traversed the frontage of the Yorkist line, and so his attack took the Lancastrian by surprise. The blow struck home between the man's hip and his shoulder, but fell against metal plate and so did not penetrate. However, the force of the blow sent the enemy staggering sideways, bundling into the man beside him. Unsteady, slipping in the quagmire underfoot, and top heavy in their armour, both of the Lancastrians toppled sideways, one on top of the other.
   Fauconberg stepped forward another pace, twirled the haft of his pole-axe, then slammed the heavy blade down on the nearest of the two fallen men-at-arms; once, twice, thrice. Every movement sent bolts of pain through Fauconberg's tired arm muscles. Even as he hammered his opponent on the ground however, Fauconberg didn't forget that there would be a man coming up to fill the gap, and he instinctively twisted the blade again and swung it upwards and to his right. As he followed the blade with his eyes, he felt it smash into something solid and, a moment later, through the narrow slit in his helmet visor, he saw the enemy billman falling backwards.

Then, in his peripheral vision, more of his own retainers flooded into view, stepping in alongside their lord and hacking their way into the Lancastrian block. The enemy, now aware of this sudden attack on the flank of their formation, began turning outwards and pushing into line. Within moments, the entire area of the battlefield became a confused melee.

There was nothing technical about the combat now. It had become a slogging match. Exhausted men hammered and battered each other, and those unlucky enough to lose their footing were simply trampled underfoot, many of them drowning in the churned-up mud and slush. The whole arena was made all the more surreal by the incessant snow that continued to fall. There was surprisingly little shouting now. Men were saving their remaining energy for the act of fighting, and the background noise was largely the sound of grunting, the clang of metal on metal, and the occasional scream of pain.

Even the more lightly armed archers of both sides were being drawn forward into the main combat now; their lack of armour now compensated for by the exhaustion of the men-at-arms and knights. The nimbler archers were more able to avoid the increasingly clumsy blows of their social superiors, and every now and then the blades of their knives and short swords found a gap in a man's harness. It was a bloody affair, and every man knew that the first side to give way was doomed, and so the combat took on a relentless ferocity.

Having felled another opponent, Fauconberg paused to gather his wits. A standard came into view amongst the press; white lions and other minor heraldic devices on a black and red field. He recognised it instantly. Henry Percy, Third Earl of Northumberland. "Northumberland!" Fauconberg yelled to nobody in particular. "Kill Northumberland!"

A billman in a badly-stained, padded jack stepped into Fauconberg's path, and drew his weapon back, ready to strike. Fauconberg noted the Percy livery badge on the man's left breast, a white disc. The Yorkist lord brought his pole-axe up and blocked the enemy's clumsy strike, twisted his weapon and threw the man's bill aside, then brought the blade of his own weapon smashing down onto the man's helmeted head. The enemy billman crumpled immediately and disappeared from Fauconberg's sight. The veteran warrior took two steps forward, his eyes locked on Northumberland's standard. Get to the standard, he knew, and he would find Northumberland. "With me!" Fauconberg roared, finding new strength. "With me! Follow Fauconberg!"

*

Howard was breathing heavily, and he had pushed his helmet visor up so that he could draw in more air. The slope had been steeper than it looked and, although they had advanced probably no more than two hundred yards, it had felt more like two miles. As he and his men reached the upper slopes of the plateau's edge, they began to come across the first bodies. Men in a variety of liveries, most covered by a thin layer of snow, suggesting that they had been killed in the early stages of the battle. The noise of the conflict had become increasingly, and disturbingly louder, but as yet there was still no sign of the men engaged in combat, such was the angle of the slope to the lip of the plateau.

Howard paused momentarily and glanced back down the hill. The entire slope behind him was thick with men, the majority of them wearing the blue and tawney-orange smocks with white lion livery badge of the Duke of Norfolk. There were at least a thousand men at his back now, and several thousand more still streaming across Dintingdale to swell the ranks behind them. Over to the far side of the road, the archer companies were being pulled clear to form-up, allowing the men with polearms to lead the way. Hobbes was there on his horse, shouting and cajoling men into position.

Turning back upslope, Howard began climbing again. The gradient began to ease, and as it did so, the bodies on the ground became more numerous, and then, gradually, the men fighting on the plateau become visible through the falling snow. The senior knight forced himself onwards a few more paces, despite the muscles in his legs protesting at the climb, and as the ground began to level out, he stumbled to a halt and marvelled at the sight that met eyes.

In all his born days, he had never seen anything like it. Through the powdery flakes of snow that fell quietly from the leaden skies, he could see thousands and thousands of men. The nearest were less than a hundred yards from him; two great blocks of them, side on, fighting grimly in a confused melee. The mass of men seemed to stretch away far into the distance until the visibility faded to nothing due to the renewed blizzard.

Away to the right, behind the block of men that were clearly on the enemy side, hundreds of other men wandered the battlefield, dazed, wounded, lost. And that field was carpeted with bodies; hundreds, if not thousands of bodies, in some places piled three or four deep. In all his dreams, he had never imagined a battlefield that looked like this.

To either side of him, his retainers began forming up, their breath fogging heavily in the air from their exertions.

"Mother of God; would you look at that..." One of them gasped. As they stood there, gaping at the spectacle, billmen began joining them on either side, crowding forward to get a glimpse of the battle they were about to enter.

Howard tried to ignore the scene of slaughter and instead focused on orienting himself to what was happening. He stared intently at the banners and standards that he could see, and soon was able to demarcate between the Yorkist and Lancastrian lines. Quickly, he realised that they needed to move at a slightly oblique angle so that they came in on the Lancastrian flank and rear.

"Alright men; you know what must be done. Follow the banners, as fast as you can. No quarter is to be given. Cut down every enemy that stands before you. Don't stop until they are all dead, or until you are." He reached up with a gloved hand and slammed the visor down on his helmet, then took a firm grasp of his axe in both hands.

"For Norfolk, and for York... Forward!"

The Rout

Sim knew something was wrong. He couldn't work out exactly what it was at first, but he knew that something wasn't as it should be. He was nine or ten men back from the front of their attack column, almost directly behind the Earl of Northumberland and his personal retainers. He, and many of his comrades from the York militia had been pushed in behind them to bulk out the numbers, and even the archers had been pushed forward, their bows slung now; each man armed with whatever blade he had carried to the field or had looted from the dead, of which there were thousands.

At first, everything had seemed to be going well. Their block of men, a couple of thousand strong by Sim's reckoning, had advanced steadily, finally making contact with the Yorkist line. At first it had seemed that they would simply march straight over the enemy. The advance had barely checked its pace on first contact with the Yorkist front rank, but then suddenly it had ground to a halt.

"Keep pushing!" Someone was shouting pointlessly.

"Push what and who?" Mundric, the young archer, had cried out in return.

It was a fair question. The men-at-arms and billmen who were in front of them, supporting Northumberland and his knights and retainers, were now fully engaged with the enemy, and the deadly bills, spears and pole-axes seemed to be flailing in all directions. There seemed to be heavy fighting over to the forward left too, as if the enemy were coming in from the side. It was barely possible to avoid being hit by a blade from a friend, never mind an enemy. There was no question of pushing anyone, anywhere. All they could do was stand in the block and wait for a gap they might fill, though both Sim and Mundric were hoping that such an eventuality would not occur. Surely the Yorkist line must break soon?

"Kill Northumberland!"

Sim heard the shout from somewhere to his forward left and a chill ran through him. The enemy had recognised who was leading this charge and were clearly targeting the great lord.

"Follow me! Follow Fauconberg!"

Those next words transformed the chill to a shiver of fear. Sim recognised the name and remembered his own near-death experience earlier in the battle. The enemy noble was still in the fight and no less aggressive than he had been at the very beginning.

"Fill left! Fill left! Widen the line!"

Somebody from the forward left was shouting orders.

Gradually, with no particular coordination, space began to open up to the left.

"Go left! Fill left!" The archer captain who had spoken to Mundric earlier was beside them and pointing over to the left flank. "Extend the line! Push left!"

Sim went with the flow, as did Mundric, and much to their dismay they found that they were now on the very flank of the block and even closer to the front. Sim could clearly see the blades rising and falling to his front and could hear the sickening sound of metal biting into flesh and bone. Away to his left he could see a portion of the Yorkist line just standing there, with nobody to fight, but then further on another block of Lancastrians engaged heavily with the enemy at the far end of the line.

Again, he got the feeling that something wasn't quite right, but couldn't actually establish the source of his disquiet. He switched his gaze between the fighting nearby, and the fighting taking place a hundred yards away, towards the far side of the plateau. The immediate fighting seemed to have settled into a grim, almost silent battle of wills. Men had no energy for shouting much it seemed, and the overarching sound was of heavy breathing, grunting, and the impact of weapons.

"What's happening over there?" Mundric wondered aloud, following Sim's gaze.

The billman studied the mass of men across the plateau carefully. It seemed that many of their own men had their backs turned towards him, as if they were facing directly towards the left flank of the battlefield. Why was that when the enemy was facing them from the right? The falling snow didn't make it any easier to see what was happening, but there was *something* happening that neither Sim nor Mundric could understand.

Sim looked at the banners and standards that flew above the mass of fighting men. He could see elaborate banners and a long trailing standard on the Yorkist side that he'd heard men say belonged to the Earl of Warwick. Amongst the Lancastrian ranks he could see the Earl of Devon's banner and various other standards of well-known Lancastrian nobles and knights.

Then, beyond he nearest Lancastrian troops, indistinct through the blizzard, Sim spotted more banners of an unfamiliar design. Red banners, bearing white lions rampant upon them. He hadn't seen them before; not anywhere in the Lancastrian camp, nor on the field this day. So, why were they apparently amongst the far block of Lancastrian troops?

A cheer went up across the far side of the field. It started gradually as a few distant voices, but then swelled to a mighty roar that came rippling along the Yorkist lines.
"Norfolk! Norfolk! Norfolk!"
"Norfolk?"
Mundric had heard the word too, and he threw a glance round at Sim, a perplexed look on his face.
The cheering seemed to grow in volume, and, within moments, the entire Yorkist line were punching their weapons in the air and joining the chorus.
"Norfolk! Norfolk! Norfolk!"
A sudden horrific realisation swept through Sim.
"Norfolk fights for York!"

Barely had he uttered the words, when the entire Lancastrian block on the left of the field seemed to stagger backwards as if on some unseen signal. At the same time, the Yorkist line began to edge forwards, stepping over the bodies of the men who had fallen earlier in the day. They came forward now, seemingly filled with renewed vigour. Sim and Mundric looked at each other with barely disguised anxiety, then back over at the left-most division of the Lancastrian army.

The men there seemed to be stepping backwards at speed now, some of them stumbling over the bodies of the fallen, and the Yorkist line was bending and curling, following them back. As the Lancastrian block stepped rearwards, that same word was yelled, over and over, by thousands of Yorkist voices.
"Norfolk! Norfolk! Norfolk!"

Sim caught a glimpse of movement to the left of the Lancastrian division and swung his gaze across the field. From the rear of the Lancastrian lines, he could see a dozen or so men hurrying forward, leading horses. As he studied the group, he realised that the horses were barded with heraldic livery and quality harnesses; the warhorses of the great lords and knights. Why were they bringing their horses forwards?

Several men at the rear of the far Lancastrian block seemed to stagger away from the crowd, looking stunned. Sim watched as one of them caught sight of the grooms and the horses. A moment later, the man began stumbling backwards, deliberately away from the fighting. Two other men followed his example; unarmoured men, common archers. Several more men did the same. It started as a trickle at first, but then he saw the standard of the Earl of Devon dip and disappear from view. And then it happened.

Like a dam bursting wide open, the entire Lancastrian division on the left broke, and Sim watched in horror as hundreds of men suddenly turned about and began running for their lives. As the Lancastrian block fell apart, a monstrous, feral roar erupted from the Yorkist ranks, and the entire enemy battle-line surged forward, weapons raised.

"Shit!" Sim gasped.

"Holy Mother!" Mundric bleated in shock.

The surge of retreating Lancastrians enveloped the collection of grooms and their horses so that they disappeared from sight. Banners that had been held high all day long suddenly wavered and fell. The steady, grim sound of the hacking battle had now been replaced with an unbelievable volume of shouting which rolled across the field from the left. It was the most terrifying sound that Sim had ever heard in his life. It was the sound of men who had thought they were facing their last minutes of life, but who had been delivered from that fate at the last moment. And now those same men were scenting victory, and their roar of vengeance rose high in the winter air. And all the while, that name was chanted repeatedly, gathering volume and rhythm with every utterance.

"Norfolk! Norfolk! Norfolk!"

What had been, just moments before, a clear arrangement of battle formations, was now a scene of absolute chaos. Men ran for their lives, all thoughts of resistance gone in the desperate race for self-preservation. Weapons were discarded, helmets too, and anything else that might impede escape. The mass of panic-stricken Lancastrian troops flooded back towards the block of men amongst which Sim and Mundric stood.

Right across the far side of the plateau, on the left flank of the Lancastrian line, more and more men were appearing along the edge of the field; men in blue and tawny surcoats with white lion badges. There were hundreds of them, and within moments probably a thousand or more. Men-at-arms and footmen with bills and spears and pikes, they were advancing like a solid wall driving all before them.
"Turn and face left! Form a line!"
Somebody was screaming orders urgently from nearby.
"Quickly now; form line! Face left!"
Sim and Mundric tried to do as they were being ordered, but all around them, men were looking about in confusion, their enemies now coming at them from two different directions.
"Rally to Northumberland! Face left! Hold the line! Hold the bloody line!"

The first refugees from the broken Lancastrian division were racing past them now. The fleeing troops, seeing that their own division was in their way, veered off at an angle, desperate to avoid the Yorkist troops in the Duke of Norfolk's livery. Only a few of them ran into the next division to join the ranks; the majority had clearly had enough fighting this day. Hard on their heels, the Yorkists came. In addition to the masses of men in blue and tawny, who were attacking from the flank, the main Yorkist line was curling round now, advancing upon the block of men where Sim and Mundric now stood. And then, as suddenly as it had happened to the furthest Lancastrian division, it happened to the Earl of Northumberland's block. Like a tower collapsing, the mass of men just fell apart, the collective sense of panic too much to resist.
"Run!" Somebody shouted.

At first, Sim and Mundric just stood and stared in disbelief as the men around them seemed to simply melt away. Sim looked round

to his right and saw that the dense crowd of men had thinned considerably in just a matter of moments. In the few seconds he had to register the scene, he saw the Earl of Northumberland, alongside his standard bearer and backed by half a dozen retainers, still facing the enemy. In the blink of an eye however, dozens of Yorkists surged forward to surround and overwhelm the group.
"Run!"

A hand clapped down on Sim's shoulder and he looked round. It was the captain of archers who had spoken to Mundric earlier. Fletcher? Was that his name? The look in the experienced soldier's eyes told Sim all he needed to know. The battle was over. It was lost. Fletcher thumped his fist into the shoulder of an equally stunned Mundric.
"Run you bloody fools! The day is lost! Run!"
They ran. They ran together, side by side, swept up in a tidal wave of humanity in a flat panic. And as they ran, that dreaded chant harassed their every stride.
"Norfolk! Norfolk! Norfolk!"

*

One moment, Edward was fighting hard for his life, the next, he found himself standing in an empty space. He had fought his way along the battle-line with his retainers to make sure he was at the point of contact where the nearest block of enemy would charge home and, having got to the point of danger, had quickly lost his pole-axe in the first encounter with an enemy man-at-arms. The weapon had done him good service all day, but after repeated strikes over the course of many hours, the haft had finally broken under a blow from a heavy bill.

From there on he had resorted to the use of his two-handed broadsword; a difficult weapon to use effectively in the press of men. Fortunately, he had managed to make some space with several well-placed horizontal thrusts and had found himself with room to use the weapon with more expansive movements.

As the long, energy-draining minutes had ticked by, Edward had managed to keep his fighting-arc clear, despatching two Lancastrians who were foolish enough to step into it and challenge him. Now, however, it seemed that he had all the space in the world. He stood there, breathing heavily, sword poised at the ready, swinging his gaze from right to left and back-again, looking for the next assailant, but nobody stepped forward. Indeed, it looked as though the nearest enemy were stepping backwards, as if they were trying to disengage. They stepped rearwards clumsily, stumbling over the carpet of bodies that covered the ridgeline. In his battle-frenzy, Edward tried to work out what was happening.

He noticed that the enemy, as well as stepping backwards, kept looking over to their left, his right, as if something at the far side of the line was grabbing their attention. The young heir to the Dukedom of York followed their gaze. Through the slit in his helmet visor, he stared towards the far side of the field. It was snowing heavily again, but through the veil of snowflakes he could see a mass of men milling around in some confusion. There didn't seem to be any great order to what he could see and, for a heart-stopping moment, he thought that perhaps the enemy had broken the Yorkist line. But then he saw the first Lancastrians begin to run, back towards their start positions.

Men were staggering over the dead who littered the ground, pushing each other aside. And then Edward noted a banner, that of a Yorkist knight, moving forward into the thick of the press. Men wearing the same livery went forward either side of it, their weapons reaching out for the enemy. A moment later he saw Warwick's personal standard moving forward amongst the mass of men. He spotted the Earl himself, sitting astride his charger and exhorting the men around him to advance. And then he heard the chanting.
"Norfolk! Norfolk! Norfolk!

Edward realised that he hadn't noticed the chant at first due to the rushing sound in his ears; something he had become accustomed to in the melee of battle. He could hear it now though; an unmistakable chorus, raised by thousands of jubilant voices.
"Norfolk! Norfolk! Norfolk!
Somebody clapped him on the shoulder.
"Ha! Look at them run, My Liege! Look at them run! They've had enough; good old Norfolk!"

With a rush of sudden understanding, Edward's mind caught up. He swung his gaze back and forth, several times, just to make sure he wasn't seeing things. He wasn't. The Lancastrian line was crumbling. A great block of them that had been fighting on the very far side of the field, pressing against the Yorkist right flank, had broken completely, and now the enemy division that was opposing him directly looked to be wavering too. They hadn't broken just yet, but they were stepping backwards with increasing urgency, desperately trying to maintain cohesion.

He looked hard right and saw his own battle-line curving round, pushing forward and driving the broken Lancastrian troops not just rearwards, but sideways into their own comrades, causing further chaos. It seemed that there were a combination of sounds filling the late-afternoon air. The underlying noise was like a groan, as if a giant was calling out in pain. That first sound seemed to be coming from the Lancastrian ranks; a sound of collective despair. Overlaid on that was a kind of collective growl from the vengeful Yorkist troops who had stood toe-to-toe with their enemy all day, and who now scented vengeance. And over everything, that blessed chant rang out repeatedly, like a mantra of victory.

"Norfolk! Norfolk! Norfolk!"

"Advance the banners!" Edward heard himself calling out. "Push them back! We have them beaten! Drive them from the field! Forwards!"

Around him, his retainers heard the cry and added their voices to the cacophony of noise, cheering their wild defiance as they surged forward towards the retreating Lancastrians.

Edward staggered forwards alongside them, knowing that this was the chance he had been looking for all day.

"Drive them back! No quarter! No prisoners! Kill them all! Knights and men of birth first!"

Again, the tidal wave of Yorkist troops around his personal standard roared out their defiance and, seemingly overwhelmed, the Lancastrian division immediately to their front suddenly broke wide-open.

The enemy turned their backs. Banners dipped and fell, and then the mass of Lancastrians were joining the crowds of their panic-stricken comrades already fleeing from the far side of the battlefield.

"After them! Chase them down! No quarter!" The young king screamed, feeling the exhilaration of victory rising within him.

Staggering like a drunken man over the mound of bodies lying in the bloody, mud-churned quagmire, Edward tried to catch up with the fleeing enemy, but they had decided that the battle was over and were already discarding weapons and equipment in their haste to escape. As he stumbled forwards, escorted by his personal retinue, he saw a standard still flying amongst the swirl of retreating enemy; white lions on a black and red field.

"Northumberland!" Edward roared suddenly, jabbing his broadsword over to the right.

The standard and banners of the Percy family flew defiantly above a knot of men who seemed to be holding firm amongst the mass of retreating enemy, some fifty yards or more over to his forward right.

"Kill Northumberland! No quarter! Hack him down!"

The collective growl that had risen amongst the Yorkist ranks seemed to grow again with even more intensity, and a surge of Yorkist troops from the main battle-line swept forwards on Edward's right and enveloped the small party of men-at-arms around the standard of Northumberland.

Edward could have wept with the joy of relief. He had done it. He had fought the Lancastrians to a standstill all day, with a much smaller army, and now his salvation had arrived in the form of the Duke of Norfolk's contingent. He watched now as men in the livery of Norfolk swept past his field of vision from the right; dozens of them, if not hundreds, mixed in with men from the main Yorkist battle-line. They were herding the enemy sideways across the battlefield, down the ridge into the wide vale that ran across the plateau. It was a glorious site.

"Chase them down!" He roared again, then, looking back over his shoulder. "Horses forward! Get the horses forward! Ride them down. Start the pursuit! Let none of them escape!"

"Aye, My Liege... The grooms are bringing them forward now."

That was good, thought Edward. Now was the time to be bold. They had been patient all day, but now was the time for boldness. He stood there, waiting for his horse to be brought to him, as he knew it would be. All the while, he watched his victorious army driving the enemy back with ever increasing levels of fury. All around him, the victorious chant continued, unabated.

"Norfolk! Norfolk! Norfolk!"

*

If Mundric had been scared earlier in the battle, it was nothing compared to the level of terror which ran through him now. He, along with the billman named Sim, were being swept along in the mad rush back down the slope from the Yorkist line. Men jostled and barged each other in their desperation to get away from the vengeful Yorkists who were already pouring down the slope behind them.

Men were slipping and sliding in the churned up, snow-sodden mud; whilst others tripped over fallen bodies or stumbled through clusters of arrow-shafts embedded in the ground. The air was filled by a constant, deafening roar of voices; the sound of fear, and the sound of bloodlust, mixing together in a terrible, thunderous cacophony.

Rather than gaining speed, Mundric and Sim found themselves becoming slowed by the ever-increasing numbers of men falling back from the ridge and into the shallow ground in the centre of the field. Breathing heavily from fear as much as from exhaustion, Mundric looked over his shoulder and watched in horror as the vengeful Yorkists came barrelling down the slope after their foes, cutting and hacking at anyone who fell behind. The unwilling archer looked to his front again and saw that the way ahead was almost blocked. Thousands of Lancastrian troops were down in the shallow ground now, jammed in as they followed its natural contours across the battlefield, like water trying to pass through a small funnel.

They would never make it before the Yorkists caught them, Mundric realised. He looked behind him again. In addition to the enemy battle-line which was swinging down and across the slope, like a closing door, the Duke of Norfolk's men had entered the battlefield from the flank and were driving straight across the plateau. As he watched the spectacle with an ever-increasing sense of doom, the young archer's mind worked feverishly.

Mundric's own village lay several miles away at the other side of the River Wharfe, and he knew the area reasonably well. He had once come to a summer fair in Sherburn via the bridge at Tadcaster, crossing the tiny River Cock by the small bridge that carried the

London-York road. In split seconds, he considered the topography of the area and realised what was about to happen.

"We need to go this way!" He gasped to Sim, as they staggered along together, and jerked his thumb towards the far slope where the entire Lancastrian army had started the day, just outside the village of Towton.

"What?" Sim asked, looking both puzzled and terrified at the same time.

"We need to go this way; back through the camp and the village..." Mundric waved his arm vaguely towards Towton.

"The road to York is this way..." Sim spluttered, not understanding.

"Exactly..." Mundric replied. "It crosses the Cock Beck, which is flooded. And the valley there is steep. It's a death-trap. Look how the crowd is blocking the way..."

Sim looked, then turned his eyes back to Mundric. His face showed despair. He could see what Mundric had seen. They were going to get trapped. The enemy would catch them soon enough. Mundric waved his arm to the right again.

"I know the way to the river through Towton. There are woods. We'll be safer in the trees..."

Sim looked across at Towton village, then back to Mundric.

"They'll ride us down..." He protested.

Mundric shook his head.

"They'll be too busy here. There are thousands of men to kill here. Why chase two men into the woods?"

Sim stared back, unconvinced, but Mundric knew in his own mind that it was his only chance of survival.

"I'm going this way..."

He staggered to the right, barged past two fleeing men, then began climbing the longer, gentler slope, out of Towton Dale and up towards the ridge where the Lancastrian forward camp had been. Sim watched him go for a moment. He noted the Percy livery badge on the rear of Mundric's smock. The archer came from Percy lands in the Ainsty, which lay just across the River Wharfe. He would know the lay of the land better than most.

A sudden surge in noise from behind him made Sim cast one more look over his shoulder towards the pursuing Yorkists. He could see thousands of men pouring down the slope, their banners flying high. Against the pale skyline, he could see several trees, their leafless branches standing like skeletons. Also on that skyline, he could see horses. Men were mounting those warhorses. He could see riders with long spears. The enemy was mounting up for the pursuit.

Sim made a decision. He wanted to live. He wanted to go back to his little smallholding; see his family again. He knew suddenly that there was only one chance of achieving that. With a spurt of desperation, he broke right and ran after Mundric.

*

Edward's horse could sense the excitement and was suitably skittish, desperate to set off at a gallop and burn up some nervous energy. The young king-to-be sawed hard on the reins to bring the beast under control as he trotted it forward through the press of men. All around him, his personal retainers closed in on their own mounts.

Edward had urged his horse forwards and to the right, to the point where he had last seen Northumberland's standard flying. Amongst the press he found that standard, lying muddy and bloodstained amongst a pile of bodies of men-at-arms and knights, many of them wearing the Percy livery. Looking down at the slaughtered men, Edward suspected, indeed hoped, that the Earl of Northumberland himself was among the pile of dead.

Some of the Yorkist archers were already trying to strip the bodies of the more noble casualties, and he had to urge them to move on.
"Leave them for the crows, lads. You can have your fill of their silver afterwards. Go, chase down the bastards who still live. The battle isn't over yet. Kill all before you; go!"
Looking up and seeing who it was that commanded them, the scavenging archers reluctantly moved on from the body pile and stumbled after their comrades in pursuit of the fleeing Lancastrian army. As they did so, a familiar voice called out to Edward.
"My Liege! We have the field, by the grace of God!"

Edward swung his horse around and spotted an armoured nobleman standing among a pile of bodies. The warrior had removed his helmet, revealing his greying hair and beard, all of which were soaked through with sweat. The man's weather-beaten face was bright red with exertion, but nevertheless, a satisfied smile was resting upon his features.

"My Lord Fauconberg!" Edward laughed out loud. "You live!"

The young pretender urged his horse towards the older warrior, though the beast shied away from stepping over the dead bodies that lay thick in this part of the field.

"Just about, My Liege; though in truth, it is only by God's grace that I am still standing. My old body is fair battered and bruised. I dare say I shall be walking like a man made of wood for a few days to come. I'm not sure I have the energy left to pursue our foes."

Edward laughed again.

"Ha! No matter, my gracious Lord Fauconberg. You have done great service this day. Your actions and example have given us this great victory. You deserve to rest, if any man does."

The old campaigner bowed his head in acknowledgement.

"You are most kind, My Liege. And God be praised, it is indeed a great victory. Though never have I seen such a bloody field."

"Aye..." Edward agreed. "Twas a fierce fight. And there will be more blood yet. We must not let our enemies escape. I will lead the pursuit. Wait here, Fauconberg. Take a drink and take your ease. This is your field. You have won this for us. So, stand here and enjoy the glory."

Fauconberg gave another dignified bow in acknowledgement, groaning slightly as he did so.

Edward turned his horse again and gestured to his retainers.

"Come. Let us pursue them. To the very gates of York if need be..."

*

"I need to walk for a moment..."

Sim was gasping as he drew in deep breaths of the cold afternoon air. He had stumbled to a walk as he and Mundric ascended the slope back up to the Lancastrian camp, his energy almost spent, his legs heavy and wooden.

That slope was littered with dead bodies; not as many as the carpet of dead on the Yorkist ridge of course, but enough to remind the two fugitives of how deadly the battle had been. The bodies in this part of the field all sported arrows; victims of the relentless Yorkist arrowstorm that had initiated the battle and triggered the Lancastrian advance that morning.

Mundric looked back over his shoulder anxiously.

"We need to keep running. The enemy horsemen will be released shortly. We need to reach the woods beyond the village before they catch us."

Sim panted as he staggered up the slope towards the more level ground.

"My legs are seizing up..."

Mundric chivvied his associate.

"We're nearly on the level again. After this it's all downhill through the village and into the trees."

The young archer cast another glance back towards the Yorkist ridge and the shallower ground of Towton Dale. The centre and right of the battlefield was just one heaving mass of men now, as the Yorkists swept the fleeing Lancastrian army down the wide draw and into the valley of the Cock Beck. The noise that came from that swirling mass of humanity was terrifying. It was the sound of a massacre. Amongst the crowd, Mundric could see more and more horsemen joining the throng. The Yorkist grooms would be bringing the horses forward from the horse-lines, ready for their masters to launch the pursuit.

"Take your jack off..." Mundric urged Sim.

"What?" Sim was still staggering along, exhaustion written all over his face.

"Take your jack off; it's slowing you down, and it's marking you out as an enemy."

Sim looked down at his mud-stained jack. Even with the filth of battle, the blue and white dye and the image of the white rose were distinct enough. He looked up at Mundric to see that the young archer was yanking the thin surcoat he was wearing over his head.

"This can go too..." The young archer grunted as he yanked it clear. "It's got the Percy badge on it..."

He pulled the surcoat free of his head and threw onto the ground.

Spurred into action, Mundric began fiddling with laces of his jack. His cold, numb fingers struggled with the knots as he fought to loosen the garment.

"Here, let me do it..." Mundric stepped in close to the exhausted billman, pulling a small whittling knife from his belt.

Sliding the blade under the leather laces, Mundric sawed desperately at the restraining bonds. One after another, the laces snapped as the blade sliced through them, until they were loose enough for Sim to pull the jack wide open.

"Right, get it off... Quickly now..."

Mundric helped the billman to yank the heavy padded garment free, then cast it onto the ground. Sim was left with just a thin woollen shirt covering his upper body.

"Better?" Mundric queried.

"Yes... Thank you..."

"Come on then. Start running again. We must get to the woods. We can walk for a bit when we're there."

Like a drunken man, Sim stumbled into a clumsy run again.

They were passing through the fields outside Towton village now, where their army had camped the previous night. The detritus and baggage of the army was spread wide across the area. The remains of camp-fires had been extinguished and covered by the snow that had fallen throughout the day. Camp followers, sutlers and servants hovered between the collection of carts and the odd tent. Grooms stood ready with their master's mounts in the horse-lines.

"What's going on?" An anxious-looking servant shouted at them as Mundric and Sim blundered through the camp.

"Run..." Mundric gasped. "The battle is lost... Run for your lives..."

A number of serving men, women, and grooms were standing within earshot, and Mundric's blunt announcement was all they needed to confirm what they had already suspected. They turned and ran.

The two fugitives were heading downhill now, towards the small collection of hovels that constituted Towton village. All around them, the people in the Lancastrian camp were coming alive to the danger. The sound of distress and fear increased in volume and intensity as the panic began to spread.

"Nearly there..." Mundric gasped, throwing a glance at Sim as they came to one of the muddy roads that led into the village. "Through the village and past the fields and then we reach the trees. The woods are thick there..."
Sim mumbled something unintelligible and continued to stumble along, splashing through the icy mud of the road.
   The sound of screaming suddenly cut through background noise of general panic that had enveloped the Lancastrian camp, and Mundric threw another glance over his shoulder.
"Shit!"
Mounted men were at the front edge of the Lancastrian camp now. The camp followers were running in all directions in a blind panic as the Yorkist prickers appeared on the ridge and urged their horses into the camp, jabbing their long spears down at anyone who got in the way.
"They're coming!" Mundric gasped. "Run faster. We need to get to the trees."
Sim did his best to pick up speed, his breath coming in ragged gulps now.
"Come on..." Mundric urged, a rush of terror shooting through his entire body. "Run faster..."

*

"Holy Mother of God! They've broken!"
Aston gaped in amazement as the entire Yorkist line suddenly surged forward in pursuit of the crumbling Lancastrian army.
All around the captain of archers, the men in the rear ranks, Jack included, stared in disbelief. After a day of reinforcing the fighting line and plugging gaps, terrified that their own front ranks might suddenly crumble, the thousands of archers bolstering the billmen and men-at-arms couldn't believe their eyes. One moment, the toe-to-toe scrap was in full swing; the next, the entire army was charging forward across the ridge and down slope.
   "They're running!" Somebody yelled. "Hunt the bastards down!"
A huge cheer went up; a roar of defiance, of victory, of revenge.

The archers in Jack's company had heard the cheering earlier; the repeated chant of Norfolk's name. The word had spread quickly that the Duke of Norfolk's force had arrived, sending a thrill of renewed hope through the army. Now, their arrival seemed to have tipped the scales as the entire Lancastrian line began to collapse in on itself.

The thunder of hooves sounded close by, and the Earl of Warwick and his standard bearer came galloping along the line, behind the archers.

"Forward men! Finish the bastards! You've waited all day for this! Forwards!"

Aston clapped Jack on his shoulder.

"Come on, lad. Forward..."

"What? Us?" Jack queried, drained as he was and just wanting it all to be over.

"Yes, us! This is where we get paid back in kind. Kill any enemy you find and help yourself to anything they have. This is our time. Come on..."

Jack allowed himself to be bustled forward amongst his fellows. Immediately, they found themselves clambering over the piles of dead that covered the entire frontage of the line. Jack cringed, knowing that his father's lifeless body was under that press of men somewhere.

The bodies lay thick on the ground for about a hundred yards, until the ridge dropped down more steeply into the wide draw of Towton Dale, and as he pounded down the slope, swept up by the crowd, Jack was finally able to see across the whole battlefield. The snow was still falling, though not as heavily as it had been a few minutes earlier. Through that veil of falling snow he could see the tens of thousands of men who were crammed onto the plateau, now being forced down into the draw and across to the left; towards the valley of the Cock Beck. The tide of movement was irresistible, with Lancastrians and Yorkists alike swirling down the shallow vale towards the steep slopes of the Cock valley.

From his position on the upper slope, Jack could see over the heads of those thousands of men further down in the draw. He could see men getting hacked down from behind, and others turning to offer futile resistance against their pursuers. Across the draw, some men were breaking away from the massive crowd being swept along towards the river valley. He could see them running back up the far slope, heading back towards the Lancastrian camp.

"Pick up the arrows as you go!" Aston was yelling from amongst the crowd of archers nearby. "Pluck the arrows from the ground and loose them at longest range into the bastards as they head into the valley. Let none of them live to fight another day!"

Despite the numbness of his emotions, Jack could acknowledge the horror that was implicit in that statement. But for the timely arrival of the Duke of Norfolk's men, it could have been him and his friends running for their lives, with the enemy also refusing to show any mercy to the defeated.

"Come on, Jack; pick some arrows as you go!"

Aston had spotted Jack again and urged him to recover some of the spent arrows that were still embedded in the ground from earlier that day.

There were plenty of arrows to choose from, but most of them were broken, having been trampled over by numerous Lancastrian charges and withdrawals. Nevertheless, Jack managed to find four shafts that looked to be in reasonably good shape. He paused after recovering the last of them to look again at the swirling mass of routed men and their pursuers. By way of experiment, Jack nocked the arrow across his bow stave, flexed his chest and shoulders and drew back the bow. He raised the weapon to the optimum angle for maximum trajectory, then let loose.

The arrow flashed away into the grey-white sky of late afternoon, and he attempted to track it. He lost it for just a brief second as it reached its culminating point, but then as it sliced back down towards earth, he picked the missile up again in his vision. He watched as the arrow dropped directly amongst the compacted crowd of fleeing Lancastrians. Who it hit, and what effect it had on them, he had no idea, but he saw that he couldn't miss, so nocked another arrow and loosed it in the same direction, and at the same angle.

"Archers to the flanks! Head to the flanks! Line the valley edge and loose your arrows downwards!"

The Earl of Warwick was amongst them again, waving a sword and shouting at the archer captains to take their men wide and begin forming up on the edge of the Cock valley.
"Come on, lads..." Aston shouted to the men around him, tapping half a dozen of them on the shoulder, including Jack, to make sure they had heard him.

They ran at best speed across the churned-up earth, pushing their way past the men-at-arms and billmen at the rear of the crush, to cross the wide draw and around the far side of the bloody melee that was taking place in Towton Dale. Eventually, hearts pounding and legs aching, the small group of men reached the far edge of the plateau, where they could see dozens of archers from other companies already lining the edge of the valley. Stumbling to a halt along the edge of the steep drop, Jack caught his breath and stared in astonishment at the scene that was unfolding below him.

In the summer, the River Cock was nothing more than a narrow beck, its waters perhaps thigh deep at worst; the watercourse meandering gently through the deep valley, crossable chiefly by a narrow wooden bridge close to Towton village. Now however, the banks had burst, with the waters swollen from the extremely wet weather of recent days. And there were several more bridges; bridges made from bodies.

Far below in the valley, hell on earth was unfolding. Thousands of men, many of them armoured, all of them terrified and exhausted, were tumbling down the steep slopes of the valley, where they floundered in the ice-cold water that filled the valley bottom. Men were losing their footing in the deep mud that could not be seen beneath the dark surface of the water, whilst others were simply pushed over and trampled by their comrades who were fighting desperately to escape the pursuing Yorkists.

All the while, men were getting hacked down from behind as the Yorkists now forced their way out of the draw and into the valley, whilst all along the valley's upper edge, Yorkist archers launched arrow after arrow into the mass target which was impossible to miss. The waters of the river were churned up and frothing as if some huge beast were writhing beneath the surface. Even more startling was the fact that the water had turned red. Jack didn't even need to think why that might be.

"Let them have your arrows, lads!"

Aston's voice snapped Jack out of his private thoughts. Obediently, he drew an arrow from his bag, nocked, aimed, then loosed. He did so without a sense of urgency. There was no need for haste. The valley was a death-trap. There was no skill involved at all on his part. The Yorkist archers knew that all they were doing was adding to the carnage which was now self-perpetuating. As Jack loosed his remaining arrows without any real zeal, he realised he was witnessing the death of an entire army in the valley below.

Eventually, Jack loosed his last arrow. Having done so, he stood there for a moment, watching the massacre of the retreating Lancastrians in the valley bottom. An order was shouted down the line to stop releasing arrows, for there were now as many Yorkists as Lancastrians in the valley, and it was nigh impossible to distinguish friend from foe. Indeed, those enemy lucky enough to have crossed the river successfully were now streaming up the hillside on the far bank, heading for Tadcaster. Even as they did so, the first Yorkist prickers descended into the valley, their horses sliding and scrambling down the steep slopes, before crossing the river over the piles of dead men.

Exhausted, stunned, and emotionally numb, Jack turned away from the valley. Slowly, not quite sure what he was doing, he wandered back across the plateau towards where the main battle had been fought. The entire plateau appeared to be strewn with bodies; a multi-coloured litter of humanity. Men were moving amongst the endless corpses, looting anything and everything of value, be that weapons and armour, coin, shoes, or even food.

Not really sure where he was going, and in something of a daze, Jack stumbled across the rough moorland at the northern side of Towton Dale. Eventually he came to the mud track that ran between the villages of Towton and Saxton, where the Lancastrians and Yorkists had established their camps respectively. As he reached the road, he paused to stare with curiosity at a group of around ten men who were kneeling side-by-side, along the edge of the track. They all appeared to be men-at-arms, with different livery badges and surcoats, and all of them were helmetless. Around them, other men-at-arms stood, weapons held threateningly, as if on guard. A knight, mounted on a grey charger, sat nearby. He seemed to be berating the kneeling men. After a few moments of shouting at them, he waved to one of the men-at-arms standing hard by.

The warrior, a grim-faced veteran by the look of him, stepped towards the first kneeling man in the line. In his hands the man-at-arms carried a pole-axe. He approached the first kneeling man from behind and, having done so, hefted the pole-axe in such a way so that it was held horizontally, with the short, wicked looking pyramid-spike on its reverse pointing towards the kneeling man.

Jack watched as the man at arms brought the pole-axe to a point of balance, tried a couple of experimental swings, then drew it back before slamming it forwards again with unbelievable force. Even from a distance, Jack heard the sickening sound of the spike penetrating the kneeling man's skull. Just a heartbeat later, the man-at-arms was levering his weapon clear of his victim's head and, released from the grip of the spike, the kneeling man's dead body simply toppled forwards into the mud.

The young archer gawped in horrified fascination as the man with the pole-axe took a couple of steps forwards so that he was standing behind the next kneeling man. Several moments later, another corpse was falling forwards into the mud. By the time the fourth man had fallen face down, Jack realised that he was watching the systematic execution of Lancastrian prisoners. The Lord Edward had given orders before the battle that there should be no quarter asked or given, especially amongst the men of birth. Now, it seemed, even after the heat of battle was passed, Edward's order was being followed through with ruthless precision.

Jack turned away from the scene of execution and stared back across Towton Dale towards the far slope where he and the rest of the Yorkist army had spent the entire day fighting for their lives. It had been perhaps six or seven hours ago, but it felt like a lifetime since he had formed-up beside his father and their comrades, under the command of Lord Fauconberg.

As he surveyed the vast expanse of the plateau, the sheer scale of this day's combat began to register. The bodies of thousands upon thousands of dead and dying men covered the entire slope on the

Yorkist ridge from one end to the other. In the odd area where the bodies lay more sparsely, the snow had settled, though it had turned a pinkish-red colour. Up on the ridge, the stark, skeletal outlines of several trees broke the skyline, and in the very centre, the banner of Lord Fauconberg stood proudly amongst the carnage, surrounded by a small group of men. Amongst the piles of bodies, heralds were already moving, locating the bodies of men of birth by identifying their coats of arms, banners and liveries.

Somewhere up there, beneath the piles of dead, lay Jack's father's mutilated body. His dead father's words of that morning came unbidden to the young archer's mind.

"Kiss the ground lad. This may be the earth where we are buried this day."

Slowly, exhaustion beginning to overwhelm him, Jack began walking back towards the spot where his father had fallen...

*

Somerset galloped across the wooden bridge, the hooves of his courser throwing great spurts of slushy snow up as they drummed the boards. Once across the river, he allowed his horse to have its head for a few more yards, then finally sawed on the reins, bringing the beast to an abrupt halt. All around him, the half-dozen survivors of his personal retinue reined in their own mounts. Like Somerset, each of them bore the marks of the long, bloody battle they had been fighting for most of the day. Their livery was stained with the mud and the blood of the field, their armour dented and scarred, the rivets already turning with rust from the relentless winter weather.

Also amongst the group was the Earl of Devon. Devon was slumped across the neck of his horse, helmetless. His skin was pale, with a blue tinge around his lips and eyes. Beside him, one of his retainers held him by the shoulder, trying to keep him in the saddle. It looked as if Devon had been badly wounded during the flight from the field, and Somerset didn't think he looked like he had much life left in him.

The exhausted duke stared back across the bridge, along the main street of the small town of Tadcaster, allowing his gaze to follow the dirty brown ribbon of mud out of the town, where it became part of the London-York road; the road that led to Towton. Even in the fading light of the day, the stream of fugitives heading back along that road was clearly visible. Most of those men fleeing the battle were on foot, but here and there he could see mounted men; knights and nobles no doubt, who, like him, had been lucky enough to get to their horses before the entire army had collapsed into chaos. Or perhaps they were Yorkist pursuers?

Somerset had been lucky; saved only by the foresight of his groom and page, and the insistence of his retainers. He shuddered in the cold evening air to think what could have happened to him. They had been in the thick of it, him and his men, leading a large block of troops against the Yorkist centre, when he had found his retainers calling out to him, to step back from the point of combat.
"My Lord, step back... You are needed at the rear. An urgent message, My Lord. We will break through here, but you must step back, My Lord. A message..."
Reluctantly, after much pleading, Somerset had acquiesced.

It was no easy thing, breaking contact with your enemies when they were just a sword's length away from you, but, supported by his retainers, he had carefully sunk rearwards into the main body of his division, leaving his men to fill the gap. Unsteadily, irritably, he had pushed his way back through the mass of heaving soldiery, accompanied by two knights in his service, until he had found himself at the very rear of the block of fighting men. And there, much to his surprise, he had found his groom and page waiting for him, along with his favourite horse; the sleek, fast, bay, rather than the big, bad-tempered warhorse that he reserved for use in combat situations. They were accompanied by several other grooms and the horses belonging to other members of Somerset's personal retinue.

"My Lord..." The groom had blurted out as soon as he had laid eyes on his master. "You must mount up... You are in danger!"
"What the hell are you talking about, boy? I *was* in danger, at the front of the battle, until I was called back here..."
The young groom had gestured urgently over to the very left of the battlefield.
"There is danger, Sire; over on the left. I see disaster, My Lord."

Somerset's irritability had only increased at that point.

"You see *what*? Are you mad? We're winning! Any moment now those Yorkist bastards will crumble, and you're wasting my time dragging me back here to..."

"Norfolk has come, Sire."

Somerset had stopped ranting abruptly at the groom's words. Seeing that his master was now listening, the groom had gone on in more detail.

"The Duke of Norfolk is come to the field, My Lord. We could see it from our position at the rear. Over on the left, his banners are lining the left side of the field, and there are thousands of men appearing on the far edge of the plateau, Sire; coming up from the London road. I fear we are to be turned , My Lord."

Somerset had turned his head in the direction indicated and, with clumsy movements of his heavy gauntlets, had reached up and dragged the helmet free from his head.

The Lancastrian noble had stared hard towards the eastern side of the plateau, beyond the divisions of his own army that were heavily engaged with the Yorkist line. Through the whisps of snow that continued to fall, he studied the banners. Devon, Northumberland, Trollope, and any number of other knights and nobles could be identified by their familiar banners and standards. But then he had seen it. The banner with its distinctive white lion. Then another, and another. And then he had noticed the long line of men appearing all along the far side of the plateau. Finally, he had realised that his own divisions on the left were peeling backwards, bending back towards him as they turned to face these newcomers. And as they did so, he had seen the Yorkist line begin to edge forwards, to curl towards the Lancastrians, rolling them up. Somerset's had felt a shiver run down his spine.

"That bastard, Norfolk..." Was all he had managed to utter as his mind finally made sense of what his eyes were seeing.

And then it had happened; so quickly, it had caught him utterly by surprise. He had heard the chanting first.

"Norfolk, Norfolk, Norfolk..."

Then he had noticed the change in the sound of the background din of battle; a kind of collective roar, building gradually until it became an almighty tumult of sound. And then his army had broken.

He had stood for long moments, watching in disbelief as the furthest Lancastrian division, and then the next, suddenly fell apart. Within moments, the far side of the battlefield was in chaos as thousands of men turned and fled for their lives, and the vengeful Yorkists had surged forward, thirsting for more blood.

"My Lord..." The groom had blurted out at that point. "You must mount up. Save yourself. The battle is lost..."
"No..." Somerset had snapped, not wanting to believe what he was witnessing.
How could the day end like this after so much hard fighting? How was it possible?
"My Lord... Please..."

Somerset had watched the unfolding disaster on the left and saw that the mass of retreating men were getting herded by the Yorkists, sideways across the field and into Towton Dale. At that point, reality had hit Somerset like a slap in the face. And so had the fear.

Somerset knew that, were he captured, he would face summary execution. There would be no ransom, no trading of prisoners, no outdated ideas of chivalry. If he stayed on the field he was a dead man. Without the need for any further entreaties from his groom or page, Somerset had mounted up, calling for his personal retinue to do the same. As the contagion of imminent defeat began to infect the ranks of his own division, Somerset and his men had broken away from the melee, riding hard for the bridge over the River Cock, and thence to Tadcaster. Their only chance of safety was to reach York before dark, warn the Queen of the disaster, and then evacuate the King from the city as swiftly as possible and head north towards the Lancastrian strongholds of Northumberland.

That had all been perhaps half an hour ago; maybe a little longer. Now however, Somerset and his small group sat astride their horses on the north bank of the River Wharfe, contemplating the speed of the Yorkist follow-up. The horses stamped and snorted, gathering their breath after the mad gallop from the battlefield.

"My Lord, we must keep on this road. We must reach York soonest. The enemy will be looking for you."
Somerset glanced briefly at his standard-bearer, who had made that last comment, then back towards the stream of refugees heading back through Tadcaster and the temporary safety of its bridge over the River Wharfe.

The Yorkists would follow-up soon enough. They would know what was at stake and do everything to eradicate their rivals whilst they had the chance. They would hack through the crowds of common men scrambling across the Cock Beck for safety, and then ride hard for Tadcaster, and then York, in the hope of riding down the Lancastrian commanders. Briefly, Somerset thought about Lord Clifford, who had been caught and ambushed just one day ago during his withdrawal from Ferrybridge. That memory helped the young noble make up his mind.

"Break the bridge down." He ordered. "Break it down, quickly... And then we ride hard for York..."

*

"Can you swim?"
Mundric turned his eyes away from the dark, fast flowing waters of the River Wharfe to look at Sim.
The erstwhile billman was staring in consternation at the murky waters, his face betraying his apprehensiveness.
"A bit... I think... A couple of times when I was younger, we swam in the Ouse, just down from the Archbishop's palace."
Mundric switched his gaze from Sim to the river, then back again.
"This isn't as wide as the Ouse..." He ventured.
"No..." Sim agreed. "But it's running fast, and it'll be freezing cold..."

It was almost dark. They had managed to get through Towton village and into the woods beyond it before any of the Yorkist prickers had caught up with them. Most likely they had been distracted by the pickings in the Lancastrian camp. The woods north of Towton belonged to a local landowner who used them for hunting. Even in winter, with few trees carrying any foliage, the woods were thick, and after a couple of hundred yards, the two fugitives had disappeared beyond the line of sight of anyone positioned on the outer edge of the woodland.

A small track ran through the western edge of the wood and curved around to the north-west, taking a circuitous route through the water meadows alongside the River Wharfe towards Tadcaster. No doubt any pursuers would explore that avenue as a priority. In order to stay away from any follow-up, Mundric and Sim had beaten a course roughly north, straight through the thickest part of the wood, heading as best they could towards the river. After what seemed like an age, the trees had thinned and they had found themselves splashing through the boggy ground that bordered the watercourse.

Now they stood at the very edge of the river, considering whether they might dare to attempt a crossing. If only they could get across the river, Mundric assured his companion, they would have a relatively short distance to travel before they came upon the village where his beloved Agnes and her family lived. She and her family would take them in and give them warmth and shelter for the night, and then the following day they could take several hidden paths across the fields and woodland towards Mundric's own village of Appleton. There they could stay, safe with Mundric's family, until the aftermath of the battle had subsided. Once that was done, Sim would be able to travel carefully back to his own village of Dringhouses and resume his quiet life of farming, and put the horrors of this day behind him.

Dringhouses lay on the main road from Tadcaster to York and, by now, the victorious Yorkists would be pursuing the fleeing survivors of the Lancastrian army back in that direction. It was too risky for Sim to head directly home. Laying low for several days would be the safest option until the Yorkist thirst for vengeance had burnt itself out. For pragmatic reasons alone, the Yorkist army would soon split apart and move on once it had mopped-up the bulk of its enemies. The only problem with all this logic of course, was the River Wharfe.

Like the Cock Beck on Towton field, the Wharf had been transformed by the foul weather of late. What could normally be crossed in a few strokes, would now take somewhat more effort, and the current would likely carry a swimmer along at a fast pace.

As they stood there in the dying light, the two men noted a large, dark object floating along in the murky water, from left to right. As it drew level with them, they saw it roll over in the swirling current. As it did so, a skeletal looking white hand briefly flopped over, and they caught a glimpse of a blue and yellow livery coat.

The two fugitives looked directly at each other, their faces betraying mutual concern.

"The enemy have reached Tadcaster." Mundric stated the obvious. "We need to get across here before anyone comes down the riverbank, looking for stragglers."

Sim glanced nervously upstream into the gloom.

"How far is Tadcaster upriver? It will be dark soon. Maybe we're too far down for them to find us at this hour."

Mundric took a deep breath.

"It's about a mile and a half I reckon. Maybe two. Not very far really. I don't really want to take the risk. I think we should swim across now and get moving. The sooner we are on the far bank, the easier it will be to find shelter and keep ourselves hidden."

Sim swallowed hard, looking at the river again, before looking back upstream towards Tadcaster.

"We'll need to swim together; go fast. The longer we're in the water, the more chance there is we'll get swept away or drown."

Mundric pointed downstream to where a large bough from a tree had been swept down the river and become lodged against a reed bed at a natural kink in the watercourse.

"If we enter the water here and strike out quickly for the middle, the current will carry us down until we hit that large bit of driftwood. If we can catch hold of it we can pull ourselves along it to the far bank. I'm quite a good swimmer, so stay close to me."

Sim stared downstream towards the large piece of driftwood, judging the soundness of Mundric's plan.

"We'll be wet through and frozen when we get to the other side." He pointed out. "With night coming upon us."

"Rather that, than dead." Mundric countered. "And like I said. It's not far to Agnes' village. Just over that ridge and over to the right. A mile perhaps; not much more."

Sim took a deep breath and seemed to come to a decision.

"Alright... Let's swim across..."

*

  Edward laid his sword across the shoulder of the kneeling man-at-arms.
"For your loyalty, your courage, and your devotion to your King, you have proved yourself worthy of this honour. Arise, *Sir* William Hastings. You shall be granted arms, and your lands in the shire of Leicester shall be increased and enriched in reward for your great service this day."
  Trying to restrain a groan as his stiff, exhausted muscles attempted to push back up into a standing position, the valiant Hastings murmured a humble thank you to his Lord and distant cousin, assuring him of his continued loyalty.
  The exhausted Hastings had fought like a man possessed throughout the day; for most of it, at Edward's side. He had saved the young king-to-be on at least two occasions; guarding his flank in the tight press of close combat. When Edward had returned to the centre of the field after shoring up the left flank of the Yorkist line following the Lancastrian ambush, it had been Hastings who had remained there with a select few men-at-arms to hold the flank contingents steady. Now, Edward turned to look about the field of battle to take stock of what had occurred here on this momentous day.
  "Glory to God on highest for giving us the victory on this Palm Sunday Field. The omen he sent us of late has been honoured. We will give thanks for this deliverance at holy service this night, and again at York Minster in the days that follow. God has judged our cause to be righteous and has given us the victory."
  He waved his free hand in an expansive gesture, indicating the group of retainers that stood in a wide circle around him.
"And you, my good friends, have given us the victory. Each of you will be remembered with glory and honour for your deeds this day."
Fauconberg, who had removed much of his armour now, stepped forward a pace, catching Edward's attention.
"There is much to be done, My Liege. What are your orders? I beg thee to voice your wishes, and we will see to every detail."

Edward smiled in gratitude.

"My loyal and courageous Lord Fauconberg; you too have done great service this day. Soon it will be dark. Let us rally our forces and bring some order to them again. We must, for exigency, camp here on this field this night. In the morning, my Lord of Warwick will continue the pursuit and summon the Lord Mayor and High Sheriff of York. And on the morrow too, we shall begin the burial of the dead. You are right, My Lord; there is indeed much to be done. But, for tonight, let us now rest and give thanks to God."

Fauconberg bowed his head in acknowledgement.

"Amen, My Liege. Amen."

Edward turned his gaze away and allowed it to sweep the field. In the failing light, much of the colour had faded, but nevertheless, the carpet of dead was unmissable. The bodies lay thick, from one side of the field to the other along the ridge where the Yorkist line had stood. Away to the right and in the lower ground, the bodies were piled even higher, for the slaughter of the enemy during their rout from the field had been extensive, systematic, and merciless. Edward couldn't even begin to count how many had fallen here. That would be the job of the heralds come the morning.

"I doubt any man has ever seen such a field of slaughter..." He murmured in a tired, almost sad voice. "Truly, this was a bloody meadow."

*

The church at Bolton, or Bolton Percy as it was often referred to in order to emphasise its manorial ownership, was an impressive structure. There had been an old Saxon church on the site since at least the time of the great conquest by William the Bastard of Normandy. In 1423 however, the wealthy manor had its place of worship fully rebuilt in finely cut stone, with the new building marked by a tall, sturdy-looking crenelated tower, and large arched windows in the Norman style.

The building had become a symbol of pride to the growing population of the village, which numbered almost three hundred souls. And today, on Palm Sunday, that church had been seen not one, but three services. The evening service, now complete, had drawn the greatest numbers. The lord of the manor wasn't present of course, and neither were a number of the young men from the village, or indeed the local squire; for they were all absent in the service of the King.

Nevertheless, the remaining inhabitants of Bolton had attended this most important of religious festivals and many a prayer had been uttered for those men absent on military service. Now, in the dark, and with the snow having turned to an icy sleet, Agnes of the Wood, along with her younger sister and brother, mother, and father, trudged from the church along the narrow lane to where their small house lay on the very outskirts of the village. Tucked away from most of the other buildings, the house lay close to Bolton Wood, whose timbers had once been donated by a long dead lord of the manor to help construct the roof of York Minster.

The lane was narrow; just wide enough for a cart. Along either side, ditches had been dug to help drain the land hereabouts, and the earth from those ditches had been banked up to form long dykes on either side, which also served as useful field boundaries. Walking with her family along the lane, Agnes dwelt silently on the potential plight of her beloved Mundric from the neighbouring village. They had been courting each other for over a year, ever since the summer fair at Tadcaster. Both families seemed to think that Agnes and Mundric were a good match, and Agnes felt that surely there must be a proposal of marriage, sanctioned by both families, in the offing come the spring.

Her dreams of potential wedded bliss however, had been put on precarious hold following the news that Mundric had been drawn to march off in the service of the Percy family and the King, as part of the ongoing dispute with the some of the country's lords in the south. At this point in time, she had no idea where Mundric might be, where he had been sent, or when he would be back. She had never even had chance to say a farewell. By the time the news of his enlistment had reached her at Bolton, he had been marched off by a local captain.

Ensconced in her own thoughts, Agnes was even more surprised than the other members of her family when the two bedraggled figures appeared out of the shadows from behind a sprawl of brambles and stepped into the road. She and her sister both gave an involuntary squeal at the sudden appearance of the two figures, and her father halted abruptly; stepping in front of his women by instinct, to protect them.

"Stand-back, strangers!" Her father snapped, eyeing up the dark figures. "What do you mean, stepping out on us like that? Who are you? This is Percy land. Identify yourselves..."

"Sshh... Master Wood, please..." One of the figures replied, his voice barely a whisper.

Agnes gasped aloud, recognising the voice immediately. She stared hard at the two figures and noted that their stance and manner did not appear threatening in any way. Quite the opposite in fact. Both figures seemed to be bowed and shaking.

"Mundric?" Agnes gasped, barely able to believe it.

"Aye, 'tis me, Agnes."

"Mundric?" Old man Wood repeated the query. "Is that really you? We were told you were gone to the King..."

"Aye, Master Wood. It is me, alright; and this is my friend, Sim of Dringhouses. We were with the King's army right enough but..." Mundric's voice broke slightly and he paused.

"What has happened?" Old man Wood asked, stepping closer. "Where are your clothes, lad? You're half naked and soaked to the skin..."

"Oh, Mundric..." Agnes stepped forward too, her voice filled with a mixture of relief and concern.

A small sob escaped from Mundric and he pushed his hand to his mouth to stop the noise. Both he and Sim were almost at the end of their physical and emotional strength.

"There was a battle..." He managed to say, trying hard to hold back the emotion in his voice.

"A battle?" Old man Wood echoed the younger man's words.

"A terrible battle..." Mundric said, his voice thick with emotion.

"There are thousands dead." Sim finally spoke, his voice shaking from the cold. "The King's army is defeated... slaughtered... We only just got away. We had to swim the river..."

"It was awful..." Mundric sobbed, breaking down now.

Agness rushed forward and took him by the arms.

"Oh, Mundric... You're safe now. You have found your way home, praise be to God."

They will chase us..." Mundric gasped.

"The enemy were hunting down anyone running from the battle." Sim explained. "They were chasing them along the York road towards Tadcaster. Mundric knew the way here, but we had to swim the river. It was so cold. And the river is filled with bodies. Bodies and blood."

For a few moments, the whole party stood there silently in the darkness of the lane as the enormity of the day's events were absorbed. Finally, Old man Wood spoke again.
"Here now; you will catch your deaths stood in the cold. Come to the house with us. Get warmed by our hearth, and we will find you something dry to wear. Stay with us tonight and tomorrow. If anyone comes looking, you can say that you were visiting us for the festival. When it's quieter, you can take the hidden tracks through the wood and across the fields to Appleton."
"What about, Sim?" Mundric asked, managing to get a grip on his emotions temporarily.

Old man Wood thought for a moment.
"He is most welcome to stay with us too. If it is as you say, then it is too dangerous to go near the York road just yet, and Dringhouses lies on that road as I remember…"
"It does." Sim confirmed through chattering teeth.
"Then you must go with Mundric, back to Appleton. Stay with him there for a few days. Wait until the army of York has moved on. Then, when things have settled down, you can return to your village quietly and unnoticed. I've seen these things before. The excitement will settle and the armies will move on and take their arguments elsewhere."

Sim nodded his agreement with the plan. Mundric had suggested as much himself.
"But now…" Old man Wood continued. "Let's get you inside and warm you through. And let there be no more talk of battles and death this night."

*

Margaret of Anjou, wife and Queen to King Henry VI, heard the arrival of horses and riders from inside her private chamber in the Mansion House. The bells of York Minister had just rung the hour when the sound of heavy hooves on the cobblestones of St Helen's

Square came to her ear; the stamping of the horses accompanied by agitated voices. She was a wily woman; nobody's fool. As soon as she registered the noise, her hackles rose, and a feeling of intense disquiet ran through her. By the time the footsteps sounded on the staircase, she and her lady-in-waiting were already standing in the centre of the room, ready to receive the newcomers.

There was a polite, but urgent knock on the heavy door. She called out for the person to enter and, a moment later, the door swung inwards and a royal page appeared in the doorway. "Your Royal Highness…" The page began nervously, his face pale and anxious. "Lord Somerset is here. He begs to see you with the utmost urgency." He paused slightly, looking back over his shoulder.
"He says it is a matter of the utmost…"
"Show him in." Margaret interrupted him.

Looking uncomfortable, the page bowed an acknowledgement, then backed away from the door and extended a hand towards it. A moment later, Somerset appeared in the doorway and stepped through it. As he did so, the lady-in-waiting let out an involuntary gasp of shock. Even the Queen, whose robustness was legendary, had to force herself to maintain a calm expression.

Somerset was in a terrible state. He was dressed in full armour, which was filthy; smeared in mud, and something else besides that had dried a dark, rusty, red colour. His surcoat with its colourful coat-of-arms was caked in the same mess and was ripped in several places. His armour bore a range of dents and she noticed that some of the smaller plates around his legs were hanging loose where the straps had broken. The duke's face was filthy too, his hair flat and unkept with sweat. He had dark circles around his eyes that spoke of a man who was approaching the point of exhaustion.

Awkwardly, Somerset performed a deep bow, and the look on his face suggested that it pained him greatly to do so.
"My Queen, there has been a battle…" He began, speaking in French, which he knew Margaret preferred.
"So I see." Margaret replied drily in her native language.
Somerset stood straight again, took a deep breath, and went on.

"We are defeated. We fought all day at a place called Towton; from dawn until dusk. Never was there a battle like it. There are thousands slain. We almost had the victory. We were so close. But at the very last moment of the day, Norfolk came to the field with thousands of fresh men, and our troops, exhausted from a full day of fighting, could not hold them."

Margaret accepted the information without comment.

"Clifford is dead. And Dacre too. Devon is dying. I have no news of Northumberland."

Again, Margaret did not respond. The truth was, she was using every ounce of her willpower to prevent herself from screaming out loud in despair. She had worked so hard, come so far and taken so much trouble, to build this army, rescue her husband, and bring the rebels to battle. How could this be? She had fielded the largest army ever seen in England. How could it end in defeat? And why had it fallen to her to fight this cause, whilst her half-mad husband lay snoring contentedly in his own chamber.

"The enemy will pursue us without mercy." Somerset continued. "We have broken down the bridge at Tadcaster to delay them, but there is no doubt they will be at the gates of York by morning. We must leave now, My Lady. We must get you, the King, and the Prince, to safety in the far north. There is no time to lose."

Margaret had already worked that one out. She thought of the spiked heads of York and Salisbury above Micklegate Bar. They would greet the young pretender when he arrived before the walls of York. Already looking for vengeance, the sight of his father's head would enrage him even further. There would be plenty of time for her to learn more details of this black day; but for the time being the only thing that mattered was escape.

Time was running short already, and Margret imagined the Yorkist lords, galloping hard from the battlefield in pursuit of Somerset, desperate to take the Lancastrian nobles and the entire royal family prisoner. If they succeeded in doing so, the life expectancy of the entire Lancastrian leadership would be no more than a few hours, she was sure.

Forcing herself to maintain her composure, she simply nodded her acknowledgement.

"I understand. We will leave within the hour. Wake the King…"

Epilogue

"Henry, Duke of Exeter."
Edward spoke the name aloud; carefully, precisely.
As the clerk scratched the pen across the parchment and the King's chief lords and ministers looked on, Edward, now Edward IV, King of England, stared into the flames of the large fire that had been banked up in this chamber of the Palace of Whitehall. He stood with his hands clasped comfortably behind his back, dressed in a velvet doublet of royal purple. He struck as handsome a figure in such informal clothing as he did in his battlefield armour. The scratching of the pen stopped, and Edward spoke again.
"Henry, Duke of Somerset."
Again, the scratching began as the scribe listed the Lancastrian noble's name on the Act of Attainder.
The Act of Attainder had been a long time in the planning. It had been inevitable of course, but it was so extensive that it had taken time for Edward to marshal his thoughts, and indeed, the names. The act would effectively declare that those listed were guilty of treason against the rightful king, Edward IV, and that consequently they would forfeit their lives, along with their titles and property. The victory on the battlefield of Towton had fatally wounded the Lancastrian cause, and now this Act of Attainder was designed to finish it off completely. Even now, Warwick was in the far north, hunting down the survivors of the clash from Palm Sunday that same year.
The scratching stopped again, and Edward spoke another name.
"Thomas Courtenay, Earl of Devonshire."
Silence.
Edward turned to look at the scribe. The man sat there at the wide desk, his pen hovering over the ink pot. He was staring down at the page, a perplexed look on his face.
"My apologies." Edward said calmly. "Am I not loud enough?"
The King paused momentarily, then repeated the name.
"Thomas Courtenay, Earl of Devonshire."
The clerk paled visibly, and his eyes flickered upwards for a brief moment, though it was clear he did not want to meet his King's gaze.
"Would you like me to say the name again?" Edward asked calmly.

The hand in which the clerk held the pen was shaking. Nervously, he cleared his throat and addressed the monarch, taking care to keep his eyes averted.
"My Liege... Please excuse my forwardness, but... but the Earl of Devonshire is already dead. He was..."
"...executed at York on the third day of April." Edward finished the sentence for the scribe. "Yes, I am aware of that. Nevertheless, his name will be attainted with all the other traitors. The attainder is not just a document of condemnation. It is also a document of confiscation. Even those traitors who are long dead will forfeit their lands to the crown. So, please... write the name. Thomas Courtney, *late* Earl of Devonshire."
Edward laid great emphasis on the word *'late'*.

The flustered clerk scratched away furiously, glad that his King had not taken offence at his temerity in questioning him. When he had finished writing the name, he refilled the pen with ink and glanced up at the king.
"Henry, *late* Earl of Northumberland." Edward continued, again with the emphasis on the word *'late'*.
The process continued.
Edward reeled off more names in a steady stream; Viscount Beaumont, the Lords Roos, Clifford, Welles, and Neville. Thomas Grey, Knight. Lord Rugemond-Grey.

This was just the beginning. Edward had collated the names of every noble, knight, man of breeding, and civil functionary that had given his loyalty to the enemy and raised troops in their cause. He remembered the ruthlessness with which many of these men, named here, had killed his father and brother. This was a war without chivalry. It was a war of total victory or defeat, and Edward intended to be the victor. He waited until the scribe had finished scratching at the parchment again. When the nervous young clerk glanced up, Edward continued with his dictation.
"Randolf... *late* Lord Dacre..."

Historical Note

As I emphasise at the end of every novel, I am not a historian. I just like to write novels about historical events; to try, in some way, to bring them to life. If you wish to learn more about the Wars of the Roses, there are many excellent books out there, written by great historians, who are accomplished at guiding one through the complex events (and equally complex family trees) of those dangerous and world-shaping times.

If you are interested in the Battle of Towton specifically, which is undoubtedly one of the most significant markers of the period, then there are two books that you might wish to take a look at as a starter. The first is quite an old publication, released in the 1970s, by William Seymour. In his 'Battles in Britain 1066 – 1547', he covers Towton in some detail, but in a sufficiently brisk manner so as not to bog one down with too much peripheral information. His narrative of the battle gives a very good overview of the main events and is a useful start point (not just for Towton, but for all the other main battles of the period also).

For a really detailed analysis, The Battle of Towton, by AW Boardman, is an absolute must. This book covers the background political context which led to the battle and discusses the issue of how many fighting men actually took part, along with the debate over casualty figures. He demonstrates how the armies were recruited and assembled and gives useful detail on the men of rank who took part, and in many cases lost their lives. He also considers some of the legends that surround the battle.

The battlefield of Towton remains largely unchanged and unspoilt. It is more cultivated than it once was, but nevertheless, the fields are sufficiently large that the panoramas are still spectacular, and you can walk the battlefield using public rights of way without difficulty. You can see the lie of the land at a glance and orient yourself quite quickly. The Yorkist and Lancastrian ridges are self-evident (The Lancastrian start point marked by a stone battlefield cross). Dintingdale and Towton Dale are easy to identify, and you can see quite clearly the 'funnel' down which the Lancastrians were pushed into the valley of the Cock Beck. Castle Hill Wood is still there, although a little more sparse these days than it once was. Also, if you drop down into the tiny little village of Saxton, you will find in the churchyard the tomb of the unfortunate Randolf, Lord Dacre.

Dotted around the battlefield are information boards that give a good narrative of the battle. The Yorkist ridge is punctuated on the right by a lone hawthorn tree, which can be seen from miles around. It is in this area that Norfolk's men arrived on the battlefield, rolling up the Lancastrian line and turning it back on itself.

As I have mentioned, there are many legends surrounding the battle and we will never know quite how much truth there is in them. I have interpreted some of those legends for the benefit of the story. I keep an open mind about the historical debates, but for the purposes of this book, several of the Towton legends served to bring the story to life.

Most historians agree about the action at the start of the battle, with the Yorkists using a ruse to encourage the Lancastrian archers to expend their arrows uselessly. Having walked the ground numerous times, I can only assume that the visibility must have been especially bad for the Lancastrians to, firstly, misjudge the range so badly; secondly, not notice the withdrawal of the Yorkist archers; and thirdly, to expend their entire arrow supply to no effect. Whatever the truth of it, we know that the Lancastrians chose to advance into an arrow-storm and begin the main battle by launching a general assault.

As for the Castle Hill Wood ambush, I have no doubt that some kind of crisis took place on the Yorkist left, as it is specifically mentioned in several sources, but I personally doubt it was an ambush in the modern sense. Even if the wood was more substantial in 1461, in the middle of winter and with an absence of foliage it would not likely have been able to hold a large force prior to the battle without them being detected by the nearest Yorkist troops. My personal belief is that the Lancastrians were able to feed a large body of men along the edge of the Cock valley whilst the two battle-lines were fully engaged. I believe that force then infiltrated through the wood and fell upon the Yorkist flank. That would have been, I believe, a big enough surprise to cause the crisis alluded to in the historical sources.

Lord Dacre was indeed killed on the field at Towton, allegedly by an arrow through his throat. There is a legend that a young boy, whose father had been killed by Dacre during the battle, climbed a bur tree (elder tree) and took the fateful shot in revenge. I suspect the latter part is indeed nothing more than a folk legend, but it does make for a good story, so I have blatantly used it within this novel.

The rout from the field probably saw as many, if not more casualties than the main battle. If you ever walk the field, you will quickly spot the topographical funnel down which much of the Lancastrian army was pushed. Even today, it is easy to see what a death-trap it must have been. Historical sources suggest that the slaughter was not confined to the valley of the Cock Beck, but that the immediate pursuit saw great slaughter all the way to the bridge at Tadcaster, where many fugitives were trapped by the demolished bridge and died along the banks of the River Wharfe.

The scene towards the end of the book which describes the execution of Lancastrian prisoners is probably one of the scenes most likely to represent the truth of what happened on that fateful day. Examinations of skeletons that have been uncovered on the battlefield points strongly towards the summary execution of men, even after the main fighting had ended, and chroniclers assert that at least forty knights were killed, including those executed after the battle.

One final mystery of the Towton story is this… Where was the Earl of Warwick on the day of the battle? Many accounts suggest he missed the battle due to being injured by an arrow at Ferrybridge the day before. However, I find it difficult to accept that such a major figure, with such a large stake in the Yorkist cause, and with a personal score to settle, would have been absent from the main event of the campaign. Clearly, he would not have been fit to fight on foot amongst the ranks, but I can see a prominent support role for him at the rear of the Yorkist army, probably mounted to aid mobility. Given the absence of Norfolk, and Fitzwalter's death at Ferrybridge, I cannot imagine Edward divesting himself of Warwick too at this critical moment, so I have brought Warwick to the battlefield in this novel, according to my own gut feeling.

If nothing else, I hope this novel has given you a feel for the period, and that it has perhaps piqued your interest in reading some 'proper history' about these dark, but pivotal times in the history of England. Whenever I visit the battlefield, I leave a mix of white and red roses by the memorial cross in memory of the men who fought on both sides; men who often had little choice about which protagonist they fought for.

I grew up not far from the battlefield, and so it has always fascinated me - I go back quite often to walk the ground. If you ever visit the battlefield, I would urge you to remember that, once upon a time, on a cold winter's day, brave men died there… in their thousands.

Also by Andy Johnson

And Kingdoms Shall Fall

The Finest Hour Series:

Thunder in May

Seelowe Nord: The Germans are coming

Bushido Dawn

Crucible of Fate